# Elephants In The Room

## Short fiction and essays

Charlene Wexler

# Dedication

Dedicated to my three adorable granddaughters, Lily, Bella, and Sage. I would also like to thank family and friends for providing material for my stories, and Anne Nordhaus-Bike and William S. Bike for helping to put this book together.

# Contents

# Foreword

For a good bit of my life, my best friend was my Aunt Nelda. Despite being 50 years apart in age, we were so in sync that she often called me her clone.

She had an enormous influence on my life, encouraging my artistic talents (introducing me to the Art Institute while still in grammar school), my mystical leanings (giving me a copy of the *Tao Te Ching*, again in my grammar school years), and my interest in astrology (we often talked about our signs).

Because she was 50 years older—and was loving and wise—Nelda frequently instructed me about what it was like as one's body aged, life changed, and new challenges presented themselves. "Nobody told me these things," she said. "But I'm telling you because I want you to be prepared."

Reading Charlene Wexler's short fiction and essays often brings my aunt to mind. Like Nelda, Char is loving and wise, and she's a warm and funny guide to how life evolves in retirement.

I met Char 20 years ago, when my husband took a job at the University of Illinois at Chicago College of Dentistry. Her husband earned his dental degree there, and he and Char have been active in alumni events for decades. Over the years, we grew from being acquaintances and colleagues to close friends.

Along the way, we discovered how much we have in common and how often we're on the same wavelength. We're both writers, we've both lived in Chicago or its greater metro area our whole lives, and we've attended literary events together and even shared the stage at a joint book signing when we both had new books out.

A few years ago, we and our husbands attended the funeral of a close friend, a retired dentist who touched many lives in the course of his 90-plus years. After the burial, my husband and I felt that deep ache that comes with grief, the kind that only seems to respond to comfort food. We headed across the street to The Bagel for a late lunch. Minutes later, who should appear but Char and her husband, Sam. Of course, we sat together and healed ourselves with the ultimate in comfort food: an array of deli favorites, savored with a goodly helping of memories and that traditional mix of laughter and tears—and chicken soup.

That's the mix you'll find in *Elephants In The Room*. Reflections on life's sadness in pieces such as Loss and Grief, Charlie Our Therapist, and The Metra Train. Touching family sagas and memories in Aunt Millie, Elephants In The Room, and A Letter to my Parents from a Woman Approaching 70. Telling personal anecdotes about how much society has changed in Band of Girls and A Day in the Life of a Chicago Teenager, 1959. And the healing power of love and food, woven into several stories but especially in Apple Strudel and Taking Nothing for Granted.

Throughout the book, Char leavens life's bleakest moments with her wry sense of humor. Her unique take on life turns brief descriptions into poignant lessons on how to really do life well: not to simply "make the best of a bad situation" but to make the most of everything that comes our way, with grace and humor. Among my favorites in this lighter vein are No More Free Pie, Into the Woods, and Battleground: Leftovers.

One of my greatest pleasures in reading Char's writing is seeing her astrology shine through in all she creates. She's a Capricorn, giving her a strong sense of duty, responsibility, and leadership. Even at her lowest point in life, after the loss of her son, she carries on and does her best. She also brings Capricorn's trademark wit, practicality, and earthiness to life's challenges (see the story Hilltop Winter for a great example). And in typical Capricorn fashion, she has come into her own in her later years, showing the world how to be fabulous, vibrant, fun, and creative in her 70s.

At this stage of her life, Char has lived, felt, and loved so much—and now she's distilling it all into fiction and essays that capture her essence along with more than a little guidance on how to live and laugh well.

My Aunt Nelda also was a Capricorn. Like Char, she weathered more than a little loss and grief, and she bore it with hard work, determination, and humor. Nelda died in 1991, so she never got to meet Char nor read her work.

But I know they would have gotten on famously, had they met.

It's my privilege to call Char my friend and my honor to share a few thoughts in this foreword. I highly recommend *Elephants In The Room*— Nelda would have loved it, and you will, too.

**Anne Nordhaus-Bike**
Award-winning artist, astrologer, and journalist
Author of *Follow The Sun: A Simple Way To Use Astrology For Living In Harmony*
Chicago, 2015

# Coming of Age

# A Day in the Life of a
# Chicago Teenager, 1959

I ran up the creaking wooden steps to the Chicago Transit Authority "el" platform, making the train by mere seconds. I had lingered too long talking to friends and having a snack before leaving Hyde Park High School for the day. My dad would be looking for me.

I brushed off crumbs from my clothes before I dropped my book on the seat next to me. Chemistry homework. "Nuts," I thought. The only subject I had trouble with. I guess I won't follow the family in the medical field. Who was I trying to kid? Like the rest of my girlfriends, I figured I'd go to college for my teaching diploma and my "Mrs. degree." And at least I didn't have to worry about the draft, like the boys who would graduate with me the next year.

The ride from the school at 63rd Street and Stony Island Avenue to 51st Street and Michigan Avenue would take only about fifteen minutes. The train lurched forward, and I almost fell off my seat. I should have anticipated the turn, as I rode this route at least three times a week.

The "clingy-clang" noise of the old steel cars made concentration impossible, but other than that, riding the el wasn't too bad. Living on Chicago's South Side in 1959, I never worried about riding the el or going anywhere in the city alone. I never even thought about rapists or crazies bothering me—although a bomb from Russia might. The Cold War was in full swing, but most things in the world were calm. Dwight Eisenhower had been a good president, but sure was old compared to that gorgeous young Senator John Kennedy who was thinking of running for president now.

There was trouble in our Jewish family. A major scandal—a divorce! After twenty-two years of marriage, my cousin was divorcing her husband. He'd had girlfriends for years, yet nobody seemed to understand why now *she* would be "doing this to the family." I never knew anyone who divorced, although I was aware movie stars did it. Still, it wasn't as traumatic for the family as when another cousin married a Catholic. My grandfather sat Shiva for him and wouldn't allow any of us to see him or his new family.

I glanced at a Black teen tapping his hands on a transistor radio. I guessed he couldn't wait to get off the train and turn it on. I could identify. The sound vibrating throughout the room from my new stereo player was one of the great pleasures in my life. I took that blue-and-silver record player with its two detachable speakers, a woofer for low, and a tweeter for high, plus my 45 r.p.m. record collection, to all the parties.

The day was a beautiful spring day. The sky was a clear blue, the flowers were just starting to peek up through the soft earth, and the first of the robins were busy pulling worms out of the ground and looking for a place to nest. Best of all, the Chicago White Sox had won their third game in a row. Maybe in 1959 we would finally win a pennant, and the World Series. Even Lake Michigan—a devil in winter, icy, cold, dark, and treacherous, was clear and inviting today. Soon the boaters will be out, I thought.

I really wished I was walking home with my friends through Jackson Park instead of going to work. On a nice day like today we typically abandoned the city bus, which turned and twisted around so many streets that it took forever before it got to our stop at 67th Street and Jeffery Boulevard.

I can just see Bart and Jeff chasing after lost golf balls in the Jackson Park lagoon. There would be many golfers on a day like this. My petite friend, Claire, with her blond ponytail, would be with Bart and Jeff. Without me there, she got all the attention. Those boys liked to tease her anyway. I always gave it back to them, while she acted hurt and innocent. Meanwhile, Miss Innocent managed to wear the shortest skirts, the tightest sweaters, and little black shoes without socks. My mother wouldn't let me get away with that. My skirts were way past the knee, but my sweaters were real cashmere, and my loafers always had shiny new pennies in them.

My heart skipped a beat when I thought about tall, thin, dark-haired Jeff with the twinkle in his green eyes. He was so gorgeous and a great dancer. My petticoats had swished back and forth as he twirled me across the dance floor at a party three weeks before. My smile turned to a frown when I realized he hadn't asked me out since.

Maybe it was because I refused to let him kiss me. It was only our second date, and mom's rule is three dates before a smooch. Or maybe he is sweet on Claire now. I hate boys! I especially hate the fact that we girls have to sit around and wait for them to call. Of course three boys you have no interest in call and ask you out, while you spend your days pining for the one from whom you never hear.

I walked off the train, stopped by the water fountain for a drink, and then walked down the steps. I felt like lighting a cigarette but was worried someone might recognize me and tell my dad. Nobody in my family smoked, which was unusual for the time, and that made it hard for me to keep up with my friends who all smoked and who could sneak cigarettes from family members.

Putting my heavy school books down, I took off my black sweater. My white buttoned-down cotton blouse and black wool skirt were warm enough for the day. Blue jeans or pants weren't allowed on girls or female teachers in our school.

I pushed back the wave that constantly fell over my left eye. It was annoying, but I kept it, because Jeff had told me he loved the way I wore my thick black hair. Page boy cuts were the style, but the waves were from my inherited curly hair that I was always fighting with oversized rollers. I once had it straightened. Never again. My hair split and fell out.

That wasn't as bad as what happened to my friend Susie, whose hair turned orange when she tried to become a blonde. She was a special friend, one to whom I could tell things I couldn't tell anyone else. We kept each other's secrets, and spent too much time on the phone every night. She loved to swim and play tennis—an athletic Jewish girl! I, on the other hand, tried to avoid exercise. Also, there was no way I could talk to her about a book. She actually believed Kafka's *Metamorphosis* was about an insect.

I slowly walked the three blocks to my dad's drugstore. Washington Park was a neighborhood in decline—not like South Shore, where we lived. The apartment buildings were shabby, and the streets were strewn with papers, garbage, and empty bottles.

The neighborhood was much different than when my dad first opened his store. The area then was inhabited by a middle class who had the money for maintenance, but they had moved on when poorer ethnic groups moved in. The beautiful old stone single-family homes, now cut up and occupied by more than one family, were starting to fall into disrepair.

My dad's store also had changed with the neighborhood. Where there once was a soda fountain was now a liquor counter. My mouth salivated at the thought of those luscious chocolate, strawberry, and pineapple whip-creamed banana splits he used to make for me. We had the milkshake machine and the soda glasses at home, but the cute little black wrought-iron tables and wooden chairs were long gone.

Unlike most of the other longtime merchants, Dad hadn't fled, saying all people needed medicine and food. He loved to be called Doc, and I secretly think he liked the freedom the store brought him. He yelled, swore, and laughed heartily there—something he couldn't do at home where my mom expected prim and proper behavior.

Boy, was I hungry. Lunch had been terrible that day. No time to go out to the restaurant across from the school, so I ate a greasy, burnt grilled cheese sandwich in the school cafeteria. Dad's store had candy, chips, and pop. I better stay away from the sauce for the chips, I thought—it was hot! My mouth stung for days after eating it.

As I came near the store, a local woman named Maddy approached me. "Miss Doc, I feel today is your lucky day. Just give me two quarters for the numbers and you'll end up with double!" She was touting some kind of illegal lottery called "policy." I never seemed to pick the right numbers. Only once did she tell me I won. My quarter became two quarters then. At this rate of luck, I figured I'd better stay away from Las Vegas when I got older—the only place in the country with legal gambling.

A large blue Rexall Drug sign hung outside the wood-and-brick building that housed my dad's pharmacy. The newly installed iron gates pushed back across the two large clear glass windows were a sign of the change in the neighborhood. It saddened me that my dad felt he needed them. The door was in between the two windows that were covered with advertisements.

The store still had an enormous glass walk-in telephone booth with a hanging telephone book and a large, heavy tarnished black metal dial phone. For a dime one could make a timed call. More money would be needed for calling the suburbs or long distance. The booth was used continually by customers who didn't have a phone in their homes, by policy dealers, and even drug dealers. In the 1950s illegal drugs were still in the underground, and generally not used by most people, but they were available to people in the know.

The black-and-white triangular patterned floor tiles probably needed replacement. They were clean, but worn. I especially loved the floor-to-ceiling mahogany cabinets behind the counter. Their small drawers with the shiny gold knobs were designed to hold the drug items sold, and those needed to make medicines. A few items like paregoric, a popular stomach medicine containing codeine, had to be signed for. Dad told me to stay away from the drawer with those items, and the drawers with contraceptives. I was told to ask another employee to take care of those customers, but he told me I could handle the women purchasing Kotex.

A loud screeching noise, sounding like a piece of chalk moving across a blackboard, made me shiver. It came from the ladder running across the track at the top of the cabinets. Looking up I saw Lucas, one of my fellow workers, pulling something out of a top drawer. We seldom sold things stored in those upper cabinets. I had no idea what was up there.

When he came down the ladder he held leeches. I jumped, and he gave me a devious grin. "They still work," Lucas said, as he walked over to the elderly gray-bearded man who had asked for them.

A marble counter went across the width of the store, crossing the liquor-and-beer counter and the candy counter and running back to the pharmacy counter. A staple on the counter was the cash register. It should have been in an antique store instead of still in use. Its ornate gold-colored metal and white marble bar over the price keys were something to see. It still was efficient, though slower than a modern one.

Not far from it, by the pharmacy counter, stood a much older item: a two-tiered show globe—a fancy cut-glass vessel containing two colorful liquids. The show globe had been a symbol of pharmacy since 17th century England. It marked the drugstore or apothecary in much the same way as the barber's pole marked tonsorial establishments. People who were illiterate needed such symbols to locate these places. Dad used food coloring to make his blue and red.

Dad also had a mortar and pestle, another longtime symbol denoting a pharmacy. The pestle was a fat stone stick, the mortar was a stone bowl, and together they were used to grind medicine.

From behind the prescription counter Dad, in his white pharmacy coat and shirt and tie, greeted me with a wave of his hand. I walked into the back room and deposited my purse and books.

"Dad, I need to put together my supplies before going up front," I said.

He shook his head and smiled. "Take what you need, but honey I won't be supplying all your friends," he admonished.

I walked along the shelves in the middle of the store collecting hair rollers, the new ball-point pens, pencils, notebooks, lipsticks, mascara, Kotex, Midol, cold cream, red nail polish, a bottle of Chanel No. 5 perfume for mom, a few ponytail holders for my sister, bobby pins, and some Colgate toothpaste.

I was sixteen and old enough to run the register, but two years short of being able to legally sell alcohol. Dad had given me a quick course on how to make change by counting backwards. Everybody paid cash, although we did give credit on the honor system. Names and amounts owed were put into a little black book, but these were accounts my dad seldom collected.

I would work from 3:30 to about 6:30 p.m., when one of my friends usually picked me up. If there wasn't too much homework on the agenda, we would meet the rest of the group at one of our hangout houses, or at Carl's for hot dogs, or Mitchell's for ice cream. The radio would be blasting with the voices of singers such as Elvis Presley and Johnny Mathis, and we would sing along.

On weekends, I helped out at the drugstore during the day. If I had something special going on in my social life, my dad/boss would let me take off. Even though I had a driver's license we, like most families in the 'fifties, had only one car. The majority of mothers didn't drive. No brother with an old jalopy in our family, so I depended on boyfriends. And, I still had my Schwinn single-speed blue bicycle for short trips around the neighborhood. Too bad it wasn't one of those new ten-speeds.

In order to get to take the wheel in my dad's year-old, olive-green, big-finned, chrome-laden Oldsmobile I had to drive my mom and sister on their errands first, and even then it wasn't very often that I found myself in the driver's seat. I was a good driver, even though I still wasn't great at parallel parking. Dad and I wanted to buy another convertible (the family had had one previously), but my mom objected. Her carefully coiffed hair couldn't handle the wind, and if it rained she would get soaked while dad tried to put the top up. Dad had the loud boisterous voice, but mom really ruled the household, so her car-buying decision was final.

My friend Jim had access to a white Chevy Impala convertible with oversized tail fins, red leather interior, and something innovative— automatic push-button windows. He said this car was so sophisticated that it was much harder to hot-wire start it—I didn't ask him how he knew that. The previous weekend, we fit ten teens in it and went downtown to the Fickle Pickle, one of the new folk/beat coffee houses.

My work in the store gave my dad time to stay behind the counter and catch up on his prescription knowledge and medicine production. When my dad went to pharmacy school back in the 1920s he learned how to mix and create medicines, some of which he still sold in the store more than 30 years later. People swore by his stomach, cough, and psoriasis concoctions.

My train of thought about my dad was interrupted when an actual train porter wearing a navy blue jacket with shiny brass buttons walked in, laughing.

"Miss Doc, get down my Jack," he said. "No more 'yes sir,' no more rocking with the rails. I got me three days off."

I brought down a bottle of Jack Daniel's whiskey, but I couldn't ring it up. We actually called the man buying it "Jack," because he loved that stuff so much he would finish that big bottle, and be drunk until he was due back to work on the Pullman trains. I was especially fond of him because one spring vacation in the early 'fifties my mama, daddy, sister, grandma and I were getting ready to board the train to Miami, Florida, when Jack appeared, impeccably groomed in his porter uniform.

"Doc, what you doing here?" Jack asked.

My dad gave Jack a big hearty welcome, but he backed away when my dad went to shake hands with him. "Not here, Doc," Jack said, making a concession to Jim Crow.

We had the best train ride ever. Jack was our personal porter. Those Pullman cars, with separate compartments, dining cars set with white tablecloths and crystal and serving delicious food, made one feel special. Though I had to admit the two-day ride did start to get boring, even with the domed car designed for landscape-watching.

I remembered seeing the water fountains designated "colored" and "white" when we first went to Florida. I had stood near the "colored" fountain waiting for a rainbow of colored water to come out of it, but the water looked the same to me, causing me to think that things were difficult to understand in the South.

Thinking about the South led me to open a bag of barbecue chips. I ate a few, reached for one of the metal pop openers, and then took a sip of Coca-

Cola from my six ounce bottle as another customer came by.

"Ms. Doc, I want a package of Wrigley gum," she said. I smiled at the sweet lady, outfitted in a floor-length flowered muumuu and a patterned scarf around her head. I didn't know her real name, but Dad called her "Jemima" because she looked like the lady on the box of pancake mix.

Unlike the nice lady, I didn't chew gum now that our new dentist found six cavities. He took X-rays, something old Doc Schwartz never did. This dentist used Novocain, so it didn't hurt so much to have my teeth fixed. He had a pretty office with cream-colored equipment, and a receptionist to help him. I still wasn't that fond of the screeching sound of that slow drill, though.

I recalled having had my ears pierced by old Doc Shore. He shook so much I thought they would never be even. So I could wear Grandma's pearl earrings now. Piercing skipped a generation; Mom's ears are not pierced. I couldn't wait to go shopping for some new long earrings.

Speaking of shopping, I needed a new dress for our high school's Sorority Sing. Figured I would go shopping on 71st Street; probably at Seder's. I had a favorite sales lady there who would bring out fashionable dresses for me. I would have loved to get a fitted bodice, but thought Mom probably wouldn't okay it—too sexy. Last time I was there, I recalled, I did see a pink nylon and taffeta full skirt dress I liked. It needed a crinoline underneath and dyed pink pumps and a small dyed pink purse to go with it. I also needed new nude hose.

Lost in fashion fantasies, I was now noshing on a Hershey chocolate bar. At this rate I will need a tighter girdle to fit under my dresses, I thought. Mom had made me oatmeal with cream and a bagel and lox for breakfast, but I had run out without touching any of the food. In fact, I had run the whole three blocks to the city bus stop. I figured one day I would miss the Jeffery Express and be late for school. That morning, the bus was so crowded I had to stand in front next to some musky smelling guy while my friends were all in the back having fun.

Still in grade school at the time, my sister had to walk only one block to school. She did complain that the teachers all compared her to me. She was hoping to get a young new teacher who didn't know me. That wouldn't happen at that school. The teachers were all on tenure and they stayed in the job forever, teaching the same thing over and over to each new class of forty-eight students.

My sister told me her stationary wooden and steel desk, third back in row five, had the name "Stu G" carved on the top. She wondered if that could be my friend. "Probably." I answered. Then I told her to look under the desk. After five years, his gum was most likely there, too.

I recalled that Mrs. Parisy was the teacher who made us write down the dumb poem about chewing gum. *The gum-chewing girl and the cud-chewing cow were alike somehow. The difference, I see it now. It is the intelligent look on the face of the cow!* We had to write that 100 times when caught with gum. Actually, that cured me of gum-chewing more than the cavities did.

The store was getting busy now in the late afternoon. The doctors' offices closed by 5 p.m., and Dad wouldn't be able to contact them to fill prescriptions, so customers were lined up in the back to get their medicine in time. Though the 5 p.m. deadline didn't really stop Dad. He knew his customers and would fix them up with medicine on his own. Most pharmacists in his era did.

Dad called out to me, saying "Mom's on the phone." I entered the back of the store to dad's desk area and picked up the black phone receiver. Mom wanted to give me instructions for dinner: chicken and potatoes are made, but they will need at least a half hour to warm up at 350 degrees; open a can of Libby peas, and a can of fruit cocktail; salad made; don't forget to mix some ketchup and mayo for dressing; oatmeal cookies for later, "and let your sister dry while you wash the dishes. She hates to wash, and you do a better job at it anyway."

We could watch one of my favorite shows, but my sister will most likely want to see the *Lucy-Desi Comedy Hour.* When my grandmother was alive we had to watch wrestling, a sport she developed a passion for at the ripe old age of 70. She was the one who taught me a host of card games, including poker.

Stopped in the bathroom, so long as I was in the back of the store. Checked my image in the mirror, careful not to trip on the mop and bucket of water. The metal wringer was a killer. With my wavy dark hair and full black eyebrows, I was sometimes compared to Elizabeth Taylor. I had just seen Paul Newman in *The Long Hot Summer*—that smile, those dimples, wow! To me, he was much sexier than Elvis.

Bummer, I thought—no visiting with friends tonight if I was making dinner. Mom was going to a fundraising meeting to fight cancer—a terrible disease in the 1950s, because virtually everyone who was struck with it died within a few months. Families kept the diagnosis a secret. The word "cancer" was akin to the word "plague." Mom and her friends worked diligently to raise funds for research. The dreaded polio had a vaccine to prevent it by then, so Mom and her friends figured that cancer could be cured someday, too.

I never learned to swim because of the polio scare, even though I lived two blocks from Lake Michigan. Summer and swimming were believed to cause the disease. Even President Franklin Roosevelt succumbed to polio. A good-looking, funny humored, red-headed boy in my third grade class ended up in an iron lung because of polio. Nothing could be worse than having to lay in that thing with only your head sticking out. He couldn't breathe without it.

I tried to call my friend Ronnie, but he wasn't home and I figured he must be out driving. He really didn't need to pick me up, since I had to go straight home anyway. There was no way to get hold of someone who wasn't home back then, so I figured I'd better wait for him to come to the store.

So I went back to the front to take care of customers, but also threw a few packs of Chesterfield cigarettes in my purse for him, and at least a dollar for gas. It was up to 25 cents a gallon, and Ron was usually short of fuel, money, and cigarettes.

Rain was now pounding against the windows, making a pinging sound. I stared at the shiny black street, being washed clean. Customers were piling in through the door, mainly to get dry, and I figured we would probably sell a few of those little plastic rain hats and umbrellas now.

That reminded me that since the grocery store closed next door, Dad added all kinds of household items such as ten-cent cans of Carnation milk, dollar boxes of Dreft soap powder, metal cookie cutters, and even some toys like Mr. Potato Head. Soon, he promised customers, he would be giving out the popular S&H Green stamps, too, which could be redeemed for gifts. The

High Low grocery store by our house had lost a lot of my mom's business since Dad upgraded his own stock.

I was snapped out of my musings by the shrill sound of sirens vibrating from the outside into the store. But nobody flinched. It was the city, and something was always happening: car accidents, fights, robberies. A few weeks ago a guy came into the store stark naked. Went up to the counter and asked for a bottle of Wild Irish Rose. Reached for his money, saw he had no pants, screamed and ran out. "Nothing exciting like that ever happens when I'm here," I thought.

Just then, something exciting did happen. Bang! Crash! Boom! Screech of brakes, glass flying everywhere, screams echoing throughout, sirens continuing to blast. The car being pursued by police never stopped until, after crashing through the front window, it reached the middle of the store.

Nobody died or was seriously injured, but five of us had to be hospitalized. The store was closed for two weeks for the damage to be repaired. Dad was relieved that insurance paid for the whole thing.

Who says 1950s Chicago was dull?

# It Was the 'Fifties

I had spent the last hour wiggling and pulling myself into the girdle, with my stockings attached to each garter; the large-boned bra, a tiny black sheath with its dropped straps; and my four-inch, black, sling high heels. With black mascara eyes, bee-hived dark hair, and red lips with matching nails, I finally emerged from the only bathroom in our apartment, a few minutes before my date rang the doorbell.

Mom turned me around and smiled. "Honey, you look beautiful," she said. "Have a good time, but remember the three-date rule: no kisses until your third date!"

It was the 'fifties, and I was seventeen and in my last year of high school, going to a fraternity party with a new beau. Like my friends, I had tried to duplicate the look of movie stars such as Marilyn Monroe and Jane Russell.

It was a time when a girl's goal in life was to get that "Mrs. degree"—the title "Mrs." before her name. Some girls would marry right out of high school, while the rest of us planned to go to college first. Jobs for girls were pretty much limited to teacher, nurse, or secretary. Any girl dreaming of becoming anything else like a doctor or a businesswoman was destined to be an old maid traveling on a very difficult, competitive road. In my circle it was expected that by your last year of college you would be sporting a diamond ring, and picking out your china at Marshall Field's.

To get our Mrs. degrees, girls in the 'fifties and very early 'sixties were expected to model themselves after the dumb sexy blond stereotype: tease as much as you could without delivering. Necking and petting were fine, but going all the way and losing your virginity, and at worst getting pregnant out of wedlock, guaranteed being totally ostracized.

Instead of worrying about our weight, my girlfriends and I concentrated on our measurements, attempting to get them as close to the ideal 36-24-36 hourglass figure that today would be considered fat. Women wore dresses that showed off those figures, and men wore pants. There was a fear of being different. The middle 'sixties would change this for teenagers, but we didn't know that then. Conformity was the norm.

We lived in a community where the women stayed home and cared for the kids and the household. Coffee klatches with the neighbors and sharing recipes were part of the norm. Couples made it on one salary, which averaged around $3,000 a year. Most people lived in apartment buildings. Houses cost between $8,000 and $12,000, cars around $2,000, gas was about 27 cents per gallon, and we paid cash for everything we bought. For the few who owned stocks, the Dow-Jones industrial average in the middle 'fifties was around 200.

Life was wonderful—and if it wasn't, for sure one didn't hang out her dirty laundry for all to see. Divorce was a blemish on the whole extended family, whose members usually lived close by, so most couples just stuck out a bad marriage for the kids, or found relief in the new tranquilizers—or the old martinis.

We spent Saturday afternoons at the movies, coming in whenever, and sometimes staying for double features. Musicals such as *Oklahoma* and

*Carousel,* and John Wayne's cowboy movies, were the most popular.

For me the only real movie star was Elizabeth Taylor. I followed her religiously from the first movie I saw her in, *Lassie Come Home,* to her last one in 2001, *These Old Broads.* As an eight-year-old with large, bright eyes and dark, wavy hair I was told I looked like her. I did at that age, and again when she was in her sixties. Unfortunately, the similarity disappeared during those years in between when Elizabeth was a fantastic beauty.

But we sure resembled each other when it was the 'fifties—another reason I love that decade!

# Band of Girls

Merle waved goodbye to Tony and snuck through the back door, quietly maneuvering down the totally black corridor leading to the industrial-sized kitchen. She stopped a second to grab two oatmeal raisin cookies. If she was caught she could just say she was hungry and came down to eat. After all, it was 12:45 a.m. and curfew was 10 p.m., so she could use an excuse.

Tony had been worried about her making it back into the sorority house on time, but she wasn't. She knew that naive little freshman Julie Ann wouldn't fail her. If Merle told Julie to come down after hours and leave the lock on the door open, it would be done. Merle had a pervasive way with the pledges who lived in the Beta Chi House. Merle was a junior and the pledges had to obey the upper classmates, especially their pledge mother. They were told what to wear, what to say, when to study, and most of all to obey. It was the way of the system for years and years,

Actually she thought Tony used being worried as an excuse. She probably enjoyed the sex in his new white Chevy Impala better than he did. He still had trouble getting her bra off. She grinned slyly as she recalled their maneuvering around the back seat. She loved the challenge, while he was worried about the police showing up.

Rules, rules, rules, boring, boring, boring. Stupid University of Illinois.

It's 1963 and they still think 20-year-old girls need curfews. *Why don't they put the immature boys on curfew too?* she thought.

The plush white carpet offered nice cover for her route through the living room and up the stairs. It was cushy enough to block the sound. Some crazy designer put white carpet and lavender furniture in a house of 40 girls. It looked beautiful four years ago.

Merle tiptoed up the stairs and quietly slid into her room. Her roommate, Diane, slept like a log—or pretended to. Nobody messed with Merle anyway, except for prim and proper Susie Bloom. Merle was thinking about running against her for house president just to take Miss Bloom off her high horse. Merle yawned, too tired to think about it now. The bed beckoned her.

***

At 9 a.m., Merle threw the pillow over her long, thick, wavy black hair in an attempt to drown out the shrill ringing of Diane's alarm. Alarms should be banned from going off on Sunday mornings, she thought.

"Damn it, Diane, shut off that f...ing alarm," Merle screamed. "It's Sunday,"

Diane turned towards her, and said, "Merle, It's Father's Weekend."

"I don't give a shit about Father's Weekend," Merle replied. "I don't have a father and my mother is running around somewhere in Europe with her current boyfriend."

"If you plan to run for house president you should participate," Diane said. "My family would be happy if you joined us—that is, if you could refrain from swearing. My mother won't be able to handle it."

Merle slowly raised herself from the bottom bunk, trying to keep from bumping her head on the boards. Her head was trying to sort out why she drank so much beer last night. It was hard to go to Kam's on a Saturday night and not drink.

She starred at Diane, who was getting dressed. No cashmere sweater and matching skirt. It was dress-up day. The fathers were coming. Diane was busy hooking her stockings to a girdle, after wiggling into the tight, uncomfortable garment. Next she put on a tight-fitting flowery silk dress and matching two-inch bone-colored heels.

"Not me," Merle said. "I'll be damned if I'm wearing a girdle."

Diane turned toward Merle, and said, "You can pull it off because you're paper thin, and you are different from the rest of us. You're exotic! I'm not sure how you got into this house."

"Legacy—my mother." Merle answered.

"I thought you were from California?" Diane said.

"My mother was raised in Highland Park, Illinois, but I am all California and here by accident," Merle explained.

Diane shook her head, bent down to pick up her purse, and walked out of the room. Merle finally got up when the chatter of the other girls and the cascading of shower water quieted down. The first thing she reached for was one of her Salem cigarettes. After taking a nice long drag, she exhaled slowly. She really missed smoking something stronger than tobacco, but she was stuck in Illinois where the alternative was a big no-no. In fact, the kids here would have no idea what she would be talking about. Like when they scan her books. No one in the house knew who Kerouac was.

Merle chose a long Indian type skirt, a tight low-cut black top, and leather cowboy boots. Her smooth olive skin was accented by a pair of long turquoise beaded earrings, and a tangling beaded necklace. Merle just loved the Bohemian look popular in California, but scorned in the Midwest.

The University of Illinois went all out for the fathers—after all, they were the ones paying the bills. The weekend featured a football game, parade, tours, and a musical. The Beta Chi house went all out with a steak and eggs brunch, early enough for the parents to drive home before it became dark. Most of the girls were from Chicago or one of its suburbs—a two to three-hour drive.

\*\*\*

Beta Chi was a small house compared to the other sorority houses, with only forty girls. The building was a lovely old house with high ceilings, marble fireplaces, and stained glass windows. When taken over some 25 years ago, it was remodeled and enlarged in order to house so many young collegians.

The kitchen was equipped with two large refrigerator-freezers, floor-to-ceiling cherry wood cabinets, and a restaurant-sized oven. The best part of the kitchen was Anne, the Austrian chef. She and her helper Marian were the reason Beta Chi had the reputation for best food on the campus, and its girls usually left the house weighing an extra ten pounds.

The good china, goblets, and silverware, plus the silver trays, all donated by two wealthy families whose members sat on the board of directors, were taken out for this special occasion. The girls, who are always in a hurry, normally use the everyday white cafeteria style dishes.

Susie Bloom burst into the kitchen. "Oh Annie, you've outdone yourself today," Susie said. "The buffet table loaded with fruit, scrambled eggs, bagels and lox, skirt steak, hash browns, and homemade strudel, cookies, and bread is magnificent. Why, you even made my favorite cookies, cherries in the snow. Our parents will be so happy."

Susie gave Annie a hug before she ran out of the kitchen to the front door, where Susie took her place as the official Beta Chi presidential greeter.

Annie brushed the powdered sugar off her apron before she turned to Marian. "That is one very sweet young lady," Annie said. "She was raised right. Always thanks us. Hope she stays president of the house."

Dressed in a proper black dress adorned with her mother's pearl necklace and half-carat studs, blond hair up in a bun, Susie looked much older than her 20 years.

She was a typical University of Illinois sorority girl of the 1960s: her dad a doctor, mom a housewife, brother a high school football hero. Susie came from one of those typical upper-middle-class suburbs, growing up in a house with three bedrooms, two baths, attached two-car garage, fenced in yard protected by Lassie. Polite, prim, and proper, she knew how to set the table, pass the salt and pepper shaker properly, sit just right, and she followed the no-kisses-until-the-third-date rule. Education was her major just in case she had to supplement the "Mrs. degree" she was working on.

Her Prince Charming needed to be from the same religion as she, come from an upper-middle-class family, and be majoring in something that would let him provide for his family. A doctor or a lawyer would be great.

Susie's infectious smile and sparkling green eyes made her a perfect greeter. Happy parents entered the house through the enormous wood-and-stained glass door. Many of them had been students on the campus some 20 years ago.

The weekend had gone great: weather perfect for the fall, and Illinois had won the football game. In fact Illinois's team was so outstanding this year that there were hopes for the Rose Bowl.

"Oh Henry, I just loved the walk down the quad," Susie's mom said to her husband. "Maples, elms, and oaks all at their height of color. What magnificent shades of crimson, yellows, and greens. It brought back so many memories."

"Marian, how can you talk about trees?" Susie's dad asked. "Dick Butkus was fantastic. That linebacker is going to take us to the Rose Bowl."

Then he sang:

*Hail to the Orange,*
*Hail to the Blue,*
*Hail, Alma Mater,*
*Ever so true.*
*We love no other,*
*So, let our motto be;*
*Victory Illinois*
*Varsity*

Susie's dad was quickly joined in song by other male alums. A winning football game could do wonders for morale.

Susie laughed as she eavesdropped on her parents' conversation.

The house filled up quickly. Chattering parents and students made it to the buffet table, and then they grouped off to be seated at the tables which were adorned with white linen cloths and crystal flower vases filled with roses.

"Where is your roommate?" Diane's mother asked in between bites of her cherry blintz.

Before Diane could answer all heads turned to the staircase where the distinctive clop, clop, clop of Merle's boots could be heard descending the stairs. Mothers and daughters were disgusted, while fathers and brothers were mesmerized by the seductive young lady making her entrance.

Ignoring Merle, Susie clinked to quiet everyone down, so as president she could give the formal welcome.

Merle gave a sly smile Susie's way before sitting down next to Diane. Merle poured herself a cup of coffee, and pulled out a Salem cigarette. Before it even hit her mouth two men offered her a light.

Diane said nothing. She was used to Merle's penchant for high drama.

Diane was shy, and never really felt like she fit in anywhere. She secretly envied Merle's confidence and her ability to manipulate people.

The end of brunch marked the end of the weekend activities. Work and homework were occupying the minds of the old and young. Goodbyes were said.

Dads said, "Study hard." "Do you need any cash for spending?" "Please try to do a better job keeping your checking account balanced. I get charged every time you over-draw."

Moms said, "Oh honey you look great." "I love that new hairdo. Your hair was getting too long and out of control." "You know it's your junior year." "That new boyfriend sounds really fantastic. What did you say he planned to be? Does he come from money? "Make sure and call once a week, and write. I love getting your letters."

\*\*\*

With parents gone, the race upstairs to remove the uncomfortable girdles, dresses, and heels began. Sweat pants outfits or blue jeans became the norm for the rest of the day. Sunday groups were then formed.

"Who is up for a game of Bridge?" Joanne yelled while holding a deck of cards in her hand.

"Count me in," came five or six responses.

"Too much homework," came a few more echoes.

"Sorry, I have a date with a new guy," Betsy said.

Heads turned her way, and conversation went back and forth in rapid succession.

"Who is it?"

"Jeff Greenberg."

"ZBT?"

"No, Sammy's."

"Judy, you were thinking of Neil Greenberg."

"He's taken. Got pinned to a girl from SDT. Lily or Lena something."

"The phone is ringing. Who is on phone duty? Some pledge is going to be in big trouble."

"Anyone want to join me in the TV room? It's time for the *Ed Sullivan* Show."

"Who is on tonight?"

"I think Tony Bennett."

"Forget it. Let me know when he has someone like Elvis, or Johnny Mathis. Mrs. Smith, our house mother is probably watching it in her room. Go join her."

"Hey, did you hear Peter, Paul, and Mary are coming to the campus?"

"Check it out. Maybe we can get group tickets. I would love to see them."

"Could be expensive."

"Dads will help, I bet." Most of the girls of Beta Chi could talk their dads into anything.

"I'm checking out the kitchen. I wonder if there is any ice cream cake left? That was delicious."

"I'll join you. Maybe I can find some left over blintz."

"Don't overdo it or Annie will lock up the kitchen again."

"Right. Last April we ate all the cookies she made for the exchange party with ZBT and she wouldn't make anymore, and she locked the pantry."

"We can't play bridge with seven people. We need four per table."

"Maybe the dummy can move from table to table."

"Smart aleck."

"Where's Susie? She likes to play."

"Caucusing."

"Caucusing?"

"House elections are right after Thanksgiving."

"Susie is a given. Who would run against her?"

"I will. Your next president will be Merle Jordan."

All eyes turned towards Merle, who continued on right out the front door, cowboy boots bouncing, and beads swinging.

"Who would vote for her?"

"The pledges. She is Pledge Mother and they are terrified of her."

"I know a few others who are also terrified of her. We better help Susie."

\*\*\*

Susie and her two best friends, Carol and Judy, sat in the meeting room discussing the coming election. Carol, the tall lanky one, lit another cigarette and leaned back in the big cushy floral chair, blowing smoke rings. Both Carol and Susie and most of the girls in the house envied her because she could eat anything and still stay thin. Judy, with round cheeks and well-stocked bosom on a short frame, munched on a bag of barbecue- flavored salty chips, and sipped a Coke.

"Why are you so worried about Merle?" Judy asked. "Nobody likes her."

"The pledges do," Susie replied. "There are 40 girls in the house. Some of them want change. Anyway I don't trust her. We need to start a campaign and line up sides."

"Susie, a house divided can't stand," Judy said as she reached for one of Carol's cigarettes. She lit it with her Zippo lighter with the inscription, *With my love, Jerry.*

Susie stared at the lighter. "The romance is cold, but the lighter is still hot," Susie said.

"Not so sure," Judy said. "I got a letter from him today. His excuse for not calling or writing was law school was really tough."

"Six weeks is a long time, especially when you actually called him," Susie said. "Think about it before taking him back again."

Furious but silent, Judy didn't answer. Susie was more conservative and prudish than Judy was.

Carol came to the rescue by changing the subject. She hated when Susie and Judy had differences. "How about we start the campaign at Tuesday night's knitting group?" Carol asked. "Merle won't go near it."

"I need time to organize my thoughts on the best way to deal with her," Susie answered. Perfectionism and planning were values she'd learned from her mother. They locked fingers on it, something they'd done since grade school when the three of them became best friends.

On the way out of the room, Judy stopped Susie. "I can't stand Merle, but she is smart, a female political science major," Judy said. "I think she will bribe some of the girls by doing their papers. I believe she helps Julie Ann with her work and Julie opens the back door for her."

"We could report her," Susie said.

"Susie, she isn't the only one coming in late," Judy said.

"Really," Susie said.

Judy stared at her. "Susie, you are my best friend going back to fifth grade, but sometimes you are so naive!" Judy said.

Susie didn't answer her. Yes she was naive. Half the time she didn't understand what her friends were talking about when they discussed orgasms and different birth control methods. She still planned on being a virgin on her wedding night and dated boys who observed the house rule of three feet always on the ground.

She and Joel had been together for over two years. She was hoping for a pinning ceremony before the end of the year. They made it through two summers, which is usually the test of a relationship when you live in different states. Joel was from Cleveland, Ohio, and she was from a Northern suburb of Chicago, Illinois.

He was quiet and serious. He wanted to be a doctor, which pleased her parents. They would have to struggle through medical school. She might have to teach some years, but that was in the future. School would probably keep him out of the Army. Her only problem with Joel was he was only five feet eight, and she was five feet six. Her last boyfriend had been six feet tall, but Joel was husband material.

JoAnne interrupted Susie's thoughts by saying, "Susie, ZBT boys are here, I think it's a pinning ceremony for Norma."

"Let everyone know," Susie said. "Time to celebrate."

Excited shouts ran through the house as the girls gathered around into a circle, passing the lit candle that one of the boys gave Susie. The tradition dictated that the candle was passed around the circle until the girl being pinned blew it out. No one was surprised when the candle was blown out by Norma. The boys from ZBT circled the house singing their fraternity songs. Brad Stone approached Norma.

"Norma you are the love of my life," Brad said. "Please accept my fraternity pin as a symbol of my love."

Every girl sighed at the beautiful romantic ceremony, dreaming of their turn at the candle. Pinning was the first step before engagement, and an "Mrs. degree."

\*\*\*

Monday morning was a busy day at Beta Chi. Forty girls had to shower, dress, eat breakfast, and get to classes. Chaos ensued, especially on the last Monday of every month when the reminder on the bulletin board said, "Ironing Lady will be here today. Make sure your clothes are labeled!" Most of the girls used the machines in the basement to wash their clothes and sometimes their boyfriends' clothes, too, but ironing was another story. The ironing lady was the most popular person on the sorority circuit.

Homey smells of biscuits baking, eggs frying, and coffee brewing were coming through the kitchen doors. This morning the breakfast tables resembled Congress, with each candidate's supporters huddled near them. Merle, who demanded attention and loyalty, actually had more supporters than Susie and her friends initially had thought Merle could gather. They now realized that they had underestimated Merle.

Judy huddled close to Susie and asked, "Do you think the parents' board of directors know about the underground newspaper Merle worked on when she was at Berkeley? We could send them an anonymous letter. Remember they have to approve the house president."

"I think that would be an obnoxious thing to do," Susie said. "I won't campaign underhandedly."

"Susie, I don't think you are aware of the things Merle is saying about you," Carol said, right before she took a gulp of orange juice.

Eyes wide open in the expression of a surprised trusting child, Susie asked, "What could she say?"

Judy didn't want to hurt her friend, but.... She tucked her legs together under her chair, twiddled her spoon, around her fingers, and said, "Things like, 'Susie is two-faced; she pretends to be everyone's friend but talks about them behind their back.'"

Crossing her arms across her chest in a defensive motion, Susie tried to talk but her heart was racing and her lips were trembling. Righteous indignation overwhelmed her. Finally she looked at Judy and asked, "Is that the way you see me, Judy?"

"No," Judy replied, "Of course not, but...."

Carol jumped up, knocking into Judy's chair as she made a hasty retreat out of the kitchen mumbling, "I have to go to classes."

Susie looked out the window. A big dark cloud formed across the sky. "Maybe we have to be more aggressive in our campaign," she said in a quiet, meek voice.

\*\*\*

A terrible storm brewed just as classes started. Umbrellas and raincoats bedecked the girls leaving the house. Chaotic traffic moved through the campus quad as wheelchairs and bicycles rolled in between students who raced against the wind and rain. Merle was one of these students.

Merle's classes didn't begin until the afternoon, so today she hurried to a meeting at the canteen.

She removed her rain coat and slid into a seat across from Myrna. Three others soon joined the group. They were a branch of the radical student group called Students for a Democratic Society (SDS), a group dedicated to the civil rights movement, the end of all wars, and social justice for all.

Jim, a big, muscular, pony-tailed guy, dropped his books on the table and shouted out, "I did it. He's coming here right before Thanksgiving."

"Jim, stop shouting and keep your voice down," Merle said as she pushed him down into a chair. Eyes turned toward their table.

"I am so excited," Jim said. "Tom Hayden is coming here."

"Who is Tom Hayden?" freckled-faced, red-haired Myrna asked in between bites of her grilled cheese sandwich.

Merle got up and said, "If you can't keep your voices down I'm leaving."

"Why are you always so secretive?" Jodi asked.

In a quiet but stern voice Merle said, "I am at this God-forsaken Midwest university instead of at my beloved Berkeley because my SDS group took to shouting out its demands for radical social changes before we were organized enough and we ended up in jail. Consequently, my parents shipped me out here." Her abortion, which was illegal even in California at the time, Merle had blocked from her mind and did not mention.

Turning towards Jim, Merle's knotted eyebrows relaxed and her pursed lips turned into a wide smile. "If Hayden shows up at our meeting I will really be impressed," she admitted.

Nora—tall, thin, and almost as attractive as Merle—tapped Merle on the shoulder. Merle twirled around to face her.

Nora flipped the ashes off her cigarette into the ashtray, looked straight into Merle's face, and challenged her with, "Why are you running for president of a sorority? In fact why are you even in a sorority?"

"Without the money and power from the parents of the dumb naive fraternity and sorority kids, our cause is lost," Merle answered with conviction.

***

Tuesday night two groups met: knit one pearl two, and boys one sex two. The larger group led by Susie met in the basement community room, while the smaller group led by Merle met in her room.

Jodi entered the knitting room. A sudden silence filled the room. "I thought you were going to the meeting in Merle's room?" Carol finally said.

"Too much talk about sex and politics for me," Jodi asserted. "Do you really think Merle has had sex with all those boys?"

"What else are they talking about?" Susie asked.

"The election," Jodi replied. "Listen I need help following instructions on this sweater." She held out her half-finished blue and white sweater.

"Jodi, we need a spy," Carol said. "Merle trusts you."

"Help me with the sweater first," Jodi said. "It's for Gary. Then I'll go back."

"Go back upstairs now; I'll finish the damn sweater," Judy said.

"OK, OK," Jodi said. "Though you might want to join me. Merle is passing out Spudnuts from the donut shop in Urbana."

"Mmmm, they are so good. That could sway my vote," Norma said as she closed her eyes and licked her tongue across her mouth.

***

The living room lacked sufficient heat for Thursday's meeting night so the young women stoked up the fireplace and brought down blankets. November and fluctuating temperatures created a combination that wrought havoc on an old house. The room filled up quickly with pajama-clad girls clutching bowls of popcorn, dishes of cookies, packs of cigarettes, and ash trays.

The crackle of the fire and the sweet smell of burning wood added to the house's charm, but not much to the comfort of the girls. November temperatures had gone from the sixties to the thirties. Thus was life in Illinois.

Susie, looking fresh and pretty as usual, conducted a normal meeting before going to new business and the election. Merle was very quiet while Susie gave her spiel about why she was running for re-election. Merle did sigh, shake her head a few times, and throw a condescending smile towards Diane once or twice.

"The house has been running smoothly this last year," Susie said. "We've had successful Mother's Day, Father's Day, and fraternity socials. More girls than we could handle rushed our house, we've made a successful bid for Stunt Show this year, and I've even convinced the Fathers' Board to forget the steak for Sunday brunch and increase the dairy. We had fun exchanges like the bowling parties, the crazy hat day, the turnaround dances, and the square dances. I would like to continue as your president."

When Susie asked if there were any other candidates, Merle jumped up from her straight-back chair. The girls in the room tensed. One never knew what to expect from Merle: a big smile and a hearty laugh could quickly become a stern, mean lecture. For a change she was dressed normally: a pair of jeans and an embroidered top.

In her animated style, Merle's dark brown eyes flashed and fingers pointed as she said: "You are a bunch of people frozen in time. Busy with boys and toys, and silly rules. There is a world out there that our generation must confront. Times are changing: no more wars, women and minority rights for equal pay, civil rights, birth control, and abortion rights are some of the issues. I want to take this sorority into the real world, prepare you for after graduation."

A small group of girls applauded, while the rest of the group just sat there wishing Merle would get off her soap box. Most of the girls still believed in Cinderella. Find your Prince Charming, get your "Mrs. degree" and live happily ever after.

It was the age of Camelot. John Kennedy was their Prince Charming and Jackie their princess.

"Thank you Merle," Susie said. "Are there any other candidates for president?" No one else stepped up to the plate.

"Election will be the Thursday after Thanksgiving," Susie said. "Any other business? Do I have a motion for adjournment?"

\*\*\*

Friday morning, November 22, 1963, all minds were on Thanksgiving vacation. Plans were made for family gatherings, and for parties with friends. The elections took a back seat. Some of the girls ditched classes and took off early. Most had to wait until the Wednesday before Thanksgiving to travel.

It was a balmy sixty-degree day. Judy and Susie walked to their education class wearing just lightweight jackets. As they stepped into Lincoln Hall a shocking announcement echoed through the classroom.

"The president has been shot! Classes are canceled."

Conversation came fast.

"What president?"

"Kennedy, you idiot."

"Is he all right?"

"Does someone have a radio?"

Susie, Judy, and the rest of the class stood around Lincoln Hall in shock and disbelief.

"I'm going to the Union. There is a television there," one of the boys said as he left the group. Susie and Judy blindly followed him.

Outside of the building students and professors were standing around quietly questioning each other.

At the Union Hall the television room was overflowing with subdued, stunned individuals.

A gray-haired lady in a flowered dress said, "I was watching *As The World Turns.* Walter Cronkite broke in to tell the nation that President Kennedy and Governor Connally had been shot. He said...."

Before she could continue, Walter Cronkite broke in on the station. "Two priests have been called. President Kennedy is dead."

Cronkite took off his glasses, paused briefly, and swallowed hard to maintain his composure.

A stunned nation immobile with despair stayed glued to the television, as the images of the day played over and over. Images that would be etched in everyone's mind for ever and ever.

Lee Harvey Oswald was arrested for the assassination of President John F. Kennedy, and then murdered by Jack Ruby. A tearful nation watched its beloved president being buried while his widow, Jackie Kennedy, and his children, Caroline and John John, stood at attention.

On Friday, November 22, 1963, Camelot died, and our nation was never the same again.

At the University of Illinois classes were canceled until after Thanksgiving. Shocked and subdued students went home by car, train, or plane. Not all came back.

One of them was Merle, who never returned to the University of Illinois. She was last seen at Woodstock in August of 1969. Susie continued as president for another year. Then she married Joel and lived happily ever after. Judy went on to law school. Diane became an activist in the civil rights movement, and the house furnishings stayed lavender for years and years.

While the Beta Chi band of girls were still in school, because of November 22, 1963, knitting parties and sorority elections never seemed to matter so much anymore. Their lives after college turned out pretty much as they had wanted. Yet the tragic event of that day gave the girls of Beta Chi, along with their entire generation, the grit to be able to handle the turbulent decades yet to come.

# Second Date

"Okay," I say. "I have many different girls. Tell me what you would like: a brunette, a blonde, or a redhead?"

"Uh, I'm not sure," he answers.

"Let's try a different angle," I shot back. "Tall, short, fat, thin, smart, or just fun?"

He hesitates.

I'm wondering about this guy. After all, we are communicating on the phone, and I can't really read him. I ask, "Who did you say sent you to me?"

"Farrell," he replies. "I'm in dental school with him, and he told me you are fixing up all his friends with girls. I didn't realize you knew so many."

(I bet you thought you were reading the beginning of a juicy call girl story. Sorry.)

I answer him with, "I'm the social chairman of my sorority, and those are the girls I am talking about. What is your name again?"

"Sam Wexler," he answers. The line becomes quiet on both ends. Sam and I went out with each other about four-and-a-half years earlier, when I was 16 and he was 19. We really didn't connect then. To me he was too serious, and to him I was too frivolous.

However, I did remember him being good-looking, even though he had a very thick head of black hair that needed cutting. He remembered me wearing a red jacket that hid my figure, and being afraid for his life because Ronnie, the male half of the couple with whom we double-dated that evening, drove like a maniac.

He breaks the silence. "I'm graduating dental school this weekend, and going into the army in three months," Sam says. "I'm not really looking for a girlfriend."

"I'm also graduating this weekend, from the University of Illinois," I reply.

"What are you doing Saturday night?" he asks. "We could celebrate together."

I think about it before answering. I had just broken up from a three-year relationship, and wasn't looking to start another one this soon. Though it sounds like he will be around only a few months, anyway.

"What the hell, why not?" I answer. "I could bring along some pictures of the girls in my sorority."

More mature than we had been nearly five years earlier, we found that on this second date we clicked much better than on the first. We went to a restaurant in Chicago's Old Town neighborhood, where I had my first taste of real Italian food, and we spent time getting to know each other.

That was the beginning of a two-year long-distance relationship. Captain Sam Wexler, a dentist in the U.S. Army, first stationed in Fort Benning, Georgia, was able to find a way to come home to visit me often. Later when he was sent to Okinawa, our romance continued through the mail, while I was home in Chicago teaching school.

We married in 1967 and still are together more than 45 years later. Still in love after many ups and downs. Enjoying retirement, and our son, daughter-in-law, and three beautiful granddaughters

Sam will tell you it all started with the tight black tee-strap dress I wore on that second date, June 8, 1964.

# Taking Nothing For Granted

He had always loved her more than she had loved him. He was the one who had waited for years. He would look at her with those hungry eyes, and would jump at the sound of her voice.

They had met while he was a soda jerk in a drugstore. He had dropped a beverage all over her, because he had been so taken by her beauty.

At first he had annoyed her. She was young, petite, barely five feet tall, never weighing more than one hundred pounds, with bright large hazel eyes, wavy auburn hair, and an hourglass figure. Charismatic and outgoing, she had many suitors. She was a tease who had the habit of keeping all her boyfriends around whether she cared for them or not. Him, she took for granted.

Her house in Chicago was a meeting place for her friends, and her older brother's friends, too; something like the salons of Old Europe. She liked to call her family's home their "Cosmopolitan Rendezvous." The family wasn't rich, but there was always plenty of food, music, and lively conversation available in her house.

Her mother, Lena, was an expert seamstress who worked for the affluent families living on Prairie Avenue and in Hyde Park, so she was always dressed in the latest styles of clothing. Lena had what they called "needle knack"— she could walk down State Street through stores like Marshall Field's and preserve a mental picture of the latest fashions. At home she would sit down at her treadle Singer sewing machine and reproduce them using cheaper material—but no one needed to know that.

The daughter had spent many a day helping her mother schlep bags of clothes and delicate antiques, generously given to the mother by those affluent families. She once had to help her mother drag a carved wooden Chinese chair on a streetcar—they certainly didn't own a car back in the early 1930s. The chair became known as the "Swift Meat Packing heirloom," as it came from the Swift home, given away when the Chinese décor fad passed out of fashion. That was something the ultra-rich did all the time.

Times like that embarrassed her, but nobody fought with Lena. She was a tough, strong-willed woman who had traveled across the ocean from Lithuania by herself at the age of twelve, and had been the head of her family ever since. In Lena's eyes the daughter was merely a daughter, and daughters were born to help their mothers work. It didn't matter that the girl was smart.

The daughter graduated from high school at sixteen, and started college courses immediately. Tragically, her father's unexpected death ended her college days, even though she had a scholarship. It was a time when it was considered more important for men to get an education, so she went to work as a secretary, while her brother was allowed to continue his schooling. For the rest of her life she resented leaving school, but without a father working money had become sparse, especially for a family that also had a crippled child.

For there was an older sister who had had polio as a baby, was confined to a wheelchair, and needed constant care. The Great Depression deepened, and times became even more difficult. The daughter no longer was out dancing or holding court in her living room, and she truly missed those carefree days.

Throughout it all, the beau she took for granted was the one who stayed around, offering a helping hand. While her other young men were having a fabulous time spending their parents' money, he had managed to make it through pharmacy school while working thirty-hour weeks in a drug store. He had never seemed smart like her brother and cousins who became lawyers. She and they had a stylish command of the English language and were up on current events, while he was always engaged in some sort of manual labor or struggling with his studies. He had little panache, but much perseverance and determination.

The country was starting to come out of the Depression, and he was a professional man with a good income who was willing to meet her prenuptial demand of moving in with her family. She couldn't fathom leaving her widowed mother and crippled sister, or their large apartment in Hyde Park.

They were married in 1938, twelve years after he had dropped a soda on her lap. She made a beautiful bride, and he a handsome groom. They probably spent too much money on the hotel reception, but his father insisted the meal be kosher. The only glitch in the party was the temperature. Chicago on Aug. 14, 1938, was a sweltering 100 degrees, and air conditioning was a thing of the future.

Life was looking up, though. President Franklin Roosevelt had improved the economy with his many work programs. War was limited to Europe, and in America we were still tooting our isolationist policies.

He was working at a drugstore in Hyde Park near their home, making a whopping thirty dollars per week, and she was back to what she loved the most—opening up her home to entertaining.

Then trouble arrived in the form of illness. He sneezed, wheezed, hardly ate, and slept a lot—but never stayed home from work. Soon he was coughing, having trouble breathing, and then his temperature started to rise and rise, and he couldn't physically make it out of bed. When his temperature hit 103, the doctor was summoned.

After examining the patient, the doctor shook his head and said, "I'm sorry, we have nothing to stop the pneumonia. The hospitals are full with respiratory disease—after all, it's the fall when the temperature fluctuates. He is better off at home. I will come by every day and check on him."

She tried to give the doctor his customary five dollars for the visit, but he waved his hand and smiled. "Forget it," the doctor said. "I have an interest in keeping him alive. He's the one who sends me patients from the drugstore— not that impossible old brother of mine who owns the place."

She stayed by her husband's bed night and day. Her heart ached. She hadn't realized how much he meant to her. He was always there, and she had taken him for granted. She tried to get him to at least sip some soup, but he coughed too much to even swallow. His skin burned to the touch, yet he shivered. She tried hard to get him to keep down the aspirin and cough syrup the doctor had left, but it was a struggle. She constantly swabbed his head with cold towels, and kept the humidifier going and the windows closed.

In the month he had been sick his robust, five-foot, eleven-inch frame became skeletal. His ribs stuck out like twigs on a tree.

She called every doctor and hospital she knew about. She had heard about a miracle drug called penicillin, but it wasn't available yet.

She could barely function. She had lost her gentle, kind, and loving father just a few years earlier, and now her husband was on his death bed.

His sister and her mother occasionally relieved her on her lonely vigil. They had already given up on him, but they volunteered because they were afraid for her health. She, however, never gave up. She knew he was a fighter who would not give in. Hadn't he fought for twelve years before she agreed to marry him?

Tiny, her little white Pomeranian who had resented his intrusion into her life, suddenly realized how much he meant to her, and spent days in the room with him, climbing all over him, busily licking his face in an effort to get a reaction.

His wife prayed while the tears ran down her face.

Her prayers were answered. The fever broke and he lived, though it took many months before he regained his full strength. She was sure it was her love that had saved him.

When he was himself again, she became a new woman, too—one who appreciated him and loved him as much as he loved her. They started all over again, with their newfound shared love for each other-a love they would pass on to their children as well.

And taking nothing for granted for the rest of their lives.

# Family and Friends

# A Night in an Inner City Hospital

"You must be kidding!" I said. "You want us there at five in the morning for surgery? We are an hour from the hospital. My poor friend won't get any sleep. Why can't she be admitted the night before?"

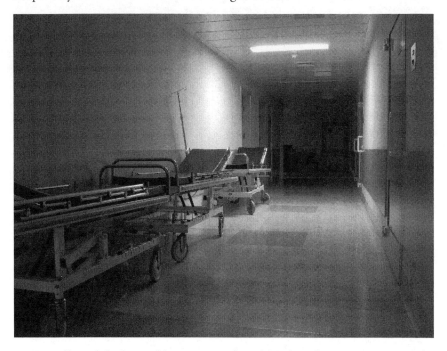

Actually, while I was blaming my friend Kasha, the patient, I was the suburban old lady who didn't want to drive through the inner city in the middle of the night.

My friend Kasha and I once lived next to each other, raising our kids here when the neighborhood was great—or at least much better than it is now. Why she was still here was beyond my understanding. All of our friends and families had moved on once the gangs had taken over. She was alone now except for me, so here I am back in my old territory ready to take care of her.

I glanced at Kasha who was sitting on her old plastic covered floral sofa, shoulders slumped down, hands folded together in a prayer position. Her small brown suitcase, ready to go, was near her tiny feet. A piece of gray hair slipped through her kerchief. In this country over forty years and she still covers her head with a kerchief. I shook my head in disbelief. Quiet as a mouse, she never complains. I guess I do enough griping for the two of us.

Her wonderful children keep calling from the West Coast. It would have been nice if they came back to Chicago to help their mother. Oh well, times have changed. Families are scattered across the world. Not like the old days when we all lived within a few blocks of each other, and busy-bodied in each other's lives.

"Medicare won't pay," was the answer from the hospital coordinator. I turned my attentions back to the phone I held in my hand. So goes our wonderful health care system I said to myself. At least Kasha was on Medicare. Money was scarce in her world. I should know. I'm always buying her things, even though it's not like I'm a millionaire.

I wasn't giving up on getting Kasha admitted early, though. I could picture the gun shots piercing the car window as we drove through deserted streets at two in the morning. "Give me the doctor's number," I said with authority.

I never got the doctor, but I did get his nurse. I told her, "I used to work in a doctor's office and I know if you put the right code in, like she may need an additional blood test or MRI, she can stay the night before surgery."

It was really a dental office I had worked in, but the code game is the same everywhere.

We hung up. Ten minutes later the nurse called me back. "Be at admitting at 9 p.m. tonight," she said.

I raised my hand and did a little success jig. Turning to my friend I said, "Now you will be able to get some rest before surgery."

How wrong I was! We were going to an inner city hospital, not the quiet suburban ones I was used to.

Admitting took forever, but that was expected. The people with the gunshot wounds had to be admitted first. In my day it was knife stabbings. Better recovery but more blood from the knife wounds. A room not far from the emergency wing with another patient wasn't particularly desirable, but we had bargained for the night, and would be gone early in the morning for surgery.

Our roommate, a shriveled-up white-haired lady in a pink flowered gown, was sound asleep in bed two. She looked like a quiet soul somewhere in her eighties, I guessed.

There was no place for me to sleep but a straight-back black plastic torn chair, but the important person in this scene was my friend Kasha. The room was in the old wing of the hospital and had seen its share of patients. Layers and layers of white paint covered the walls, and the beds had the creaky old cranks on them. The halls had that old hospital smell, somewhere between bleach and vomit. The outside lights shimmered through the window shade. Occasionally there was a glowing blue dome, signifying a police car, or a staccato siren indicating an ambulance. For the few thousand a night it was costing it could have nicer furniture and cleaner floors, but the government was paying.

Oh well. Five hours to sleep. I curled up on the chair and Kasha lay back in the bed. I threw my coat over me to help keep from shivering. My hands were like the icicles hanging outside the window. I sat on them using my fattest and warmest part to keep them from turning blue. Why they keep hospitals so cold is beyond me.

Two minutes later a barrage of doctors proceeded to examine, question, and take blood from Kasha. As I watched the orderly poke the long sharp needle into her vein for the third time I started to feel nauseated. I am a chicken when needles come near me.

Finally they left, and the nurse came in with meds, a blood pressure machine, and was ready to weigh and measure Kasha and ask her questions. I was proud of my friend. Only two days into the New Year and Kasha actually gave the date 2015 as the answer to, "What year is it?" I would have failed that question.

"Shut those doors. Nobody leave the room." Blue uniforms, shiny badges, and gun holsters paced down the corridors, as police officers shouted orders. The outside city tumult suddenly came inside. A small group of policemen combed the hospital in search of a heroin addict who had gone crazy in the emergency room. Two doctors tried to hold him down, but he escaped through the building. Five policemen finally caught and subdued him. Powerful drug, that heroin.

Four hours left to rest.

The shouting from a patient down the hall became louder and louder: "Gail, Gail, Gail." Closing the door didn't help. Soon we had a chorus of shouting from patient's rooms. "God damn it shut up." another patient started yelling, and then someone visiting ran down the hall screaming, "Mother F***** I'll kill you if you don't shut the F*** up." Since the police were still around the nurses used them to calm down the shouters.

We totally ignored the code blue alarm over the intercom, as it referred to a room down the hall, not ours.

I felt a wave of sympathy for Kasha. She looked pale and tired, as she twisted and turned in the bed. At least she had a bed, as opposed to this totally uncomfortable chair.

Two hours left before surgery and finally all was quiet. Or was it? The sweet old lady next to us who had been sleeping through everything with only an occasional snore suddenly came alive.

"Please, please get me a priest," She kept repeating in a squeaky soft but pleading voice. I called the nurses for her, and for me.

The nurses tried hard to quiet her down with, "It's okay honey. You don't need a priest; you're not dying. In fact you are scheduled to go home tomorrow."

This did not help. The sweet old lady suddenly became very agitated. She popped straight up in bed and shouted, "I want a priest now!"

It took about a half an hour before a tall skinny black robed priest appeared. He looked about ten years old to me, but so did most of the doctors. He pulled the curtains between us, and in a gentle concerned tone of voice he told the woman, "The doctors have told me that you are in no danger of dying, but if you wish confession I will be happy to listen."

The poor priest had no idea what he was in for.

My sweet little old lady proceeded with, "I wronged my husband before he died. For years I cheated on him. I did unthinkable things with men like…."

Just when the story was getting good, the priest stopped her. "You don't have to tell me anymore. You are absolved. God loves you."

"No Father, I must confess to you. I have been guilty for years. I loved sex, and my husband didn't."

Kasha was sleeping and I was sliding down in my chair feeling guilty. I always thought confession was done in the strictest confidence.

The gurney came for my friend and we had to leave this interesting floor of the city hospital, and never found out if the priest received a sex education that early morning.

My friend got to sleep during her six hour surgery. I didn't get to rest until I knew she was okay. My head ached and my heart raced from lack of sleep and from worry. Out of surgery Kasha was put on a very special floor far from the emergency wing. Silence echoed through the halls except for the occasional tap of shoes or medical carts. There was actually a lounge chair in the room for me to lie on. As I settled in next to her bed I thought, "Maybe we would be able to sleep through the night."

Then again, we were still in a city hospital!

# Apple Strudel

One step inside the Austrian pastry shop and I was overwhelmed by the sweet, spicy scent of bakery goods. My eyes opened wide, my mouth watered, and my tongue licked my lips in anticipation of biting into a delicious piece of sugary cinnamon apple strudel.

My mind, however, traveled back in time.

The kitchen in my memory was huge—but I was small back in the 1940s, so maybe it really wasn't. I do know it was very colorful: red and yellow tiles decorated the walls, which made the room warm and inviting, and the metal-edged table with the accidental cut from my dad's saw was also a bright red. The white counters were busy with appliances: the stainless mixer, four-slice toaster, and tin bread box came to mind.

The electric stove was a wonder for the times. Not my mother but my dad had purchased it; he liked to buy every new gadget. Actually, I hated the stove.

I recalled how sore my hand became from a burn I obtained on it—that burn hurt worse than when I touched the radiator.

I can't remember if there were curtains on the window over the cast-iron porcelain sink—maybe because I loved to watch the radiant morning sun strike the glass in a rainbow pattern of blue, orange, and violet, as it poked around the enormous ancient oak tree outside. On a hot summer day, a fuzzy-tailed gray squirrel or a bright feathered bird might be perched on one of the tree limbs. The window could be opened, so we not only cooled down, but listened to the sounds coming from the outside world.

Gram, with her silver-gray hair pulled back with bobby pins, her long pink house dress dotted by tiny flowers throughout, was busy working by the time I got up and dressed. I could hear the sound of pots and pans and the opening and shutting of cabinets as I entered the room.

It was early Friday morning, which was cooking and baking day at our home, and I was ready. My small wooden cutting board, my petite wood rolling pin with the red handles, and the pink flowered bowl were sitting at my end of the table. My little yellow apron with the blue sashes was waiting on the chair for me. While tying it, Gram pulled me close to her full soft body and hugged me. She called me "mein kin," which was Yiddish for "my special child."

At home she always spoke a mixture of English and Yiddish, but when we were out with strangers she could talk just English. Mom said before Grandma became an old lady in her 60s she actually wore business clothes and owned a store where she made dresses and hats. I wouldn't like that grandma. The one I had now was perfect.

When she smiled at me, I started to laugh because her smooth, white skin around her mouth was sunken. I knew why. Her teeth were still sitting in a glass on her dresser. I saw them there. My mom said I shouldn't laugh at Gram because she sometimes forgot things. I knew her better than mom. She didn't forget her teeth. She just didn't like wearing them, and she had stronger gums than anyone in the world.

Tiny, our furry white Pomeranian with the bright black eyes, was stationed under the table near my chair in anticipation of dropped food— which usually ended up on his fur, making him sticky, too. He was mom's dog before I was born, so he was getting slow.

The strudel dough was already mixed and sitting in Gram's extra-large, white porcelain bowl. I just can't remember what ingredients made that dough, but I definitely remember what we did with it—we kneaded it.

Grandma's smooth, soft white hands took a chunk of dough and put it into my bowl. I climbed up on the metal chair with the wide red vinyl cushion, and held out my hands for the inspection. Her rule was that I had to have clean hands before I could help. I remembered to wash them with mom's special perfumed Dove soap bar before coming into the kitchen. One finger wasn't sparkling clean because it still had some green paint on it from the other day when I was helping dad make the summer chairs look like new.

Gram checked behind my ears to make sure the tiny diamond earrings she gave me when I got my ears pierced were secure. We didn't want to lose one in the batter like in the book, *Homer Price,* especially since the earrings once belonged to her mother.

My dark brown eyes watched Gram work with her dough on the cutting board, and my hands tried to follow with my portion. First, she pushed the dough down and out, and then pulled it back. My hands and piece of dough always became much stickier than Gram's, so I had to add flour on the board, and stop several times to wash. I had a habit of pushing my black wavy curls off of my face while my head leaned down so sometimes my hair also became sticky, and I had to take another break, and sometimes I needed a break to get some milk to drink, or to go to the bathroom. Gram never needed a break.

Actually, that wasn't entirely true. She did take time to make a glass of tea. I liked to hear the red tea kettle whistle when the water was boiled and ready, but I really didn't enjoy drinking tea, even when Gram added a couple of sugar cubes to it.

The hard part came after the kneading. It was the waiting time. The dough was put in clean bowls, covered by a cotton cloth, and left to rise. It fascinated me that something non-living could grow to be twice its original size.

Grandma watched me closely, because four-year-old me had been known to sneak a peek under the cloth to see if the dough was ready, even though I was told to wait until the small hand on the clock reached eleven. I couldn't tell time well, but I liked the black and white cat clock on the wall with its bright moving eyes, and long black tail.

While we waited for the dough to rise, Gram cut the apples. She took her small sharp black paring knife, and in a quick circular motion the skins on the apples were made into bracelets for me. Cutting was too dangerous for my little hands, so mixing the cut apples with the sugar, cinnamon, raisons, flour, and butter became my job. I managed to nibble on some of the apples and raisins, while Grandma pretended to not see me doing it.

Finally, the dough was ready and the fun began. Rolling, and rolling, and rolling the dough was my favorite. "Thin as tissue-paper," Gram kept telling me. My dough always ended up with holes in it, but we used it anyway. Covering the apple mix with thin sheets of pastry and putting the concoction on the cookie tray and into the oven was the last job until the timer button chimed, and we could feast.

In those days, food and love went together. Women stayed home, cooked, cleaned, and watched the kids. A woman who also was a good baker was famous among her family members and neighbors.

My days in the kitchen with Gram were not only a labor of love, but a chance to master skills that had been passed on through generations, and a way to learn about my family history. That continues today; my grandchildren learn to make Great-Grandma Ida's banana cake, Great-Grandmother Edna's cherries in the snow, and Great-Great-Grandmother Lena's strudel.

My mouth still waters for the taste of that sugary cinnamon apple strudel Gram and I baked together. I've never tasted strudel that good anywhere, not even one in this Vienna pastry shop. And I've certainly never at any other time or place had strudel that was so meaningful as that baked with Gram's love.

# Aunt Millie

"Used to him? You must be kidding. You won't break up with someone you don't love because you are so used to him being around? Hell, honey, you can get used to a wart on your ass if it's there long enough."

That was my Aunt Millie talking. She knew how to get to the heart of a problem. No bull. Just tell it like it is.

I watched my prim and proper mother turn red with embarrassment and anger many times. She could handle most things, but not her sister-in-law Millie. My own sister and I smiled at each other whenever Aunt Millie was around, however. We loved having our own non-conformist—a real life Auntie Mame.

To start with, our Aunt Millie was different than the other family members in our upper middle class Chicago family—we even had a Federal judge in our lineage. Millie came from a rural New York farm family.

By the time she got to Chicago she was no longer a farm girl. At 29, she had traveled around the country, experiencing things we only read about. She was street wise beyond her years.

Horrified by her outfits (although she was really ahead of her time when she put a pink sweater together with a red skirt), the women in the family directed her to various Chicago stores' designer departments, and she soon became more stylish than anyone else. Of course, her long black hair and tall, slim figure helped. Oh, how I loved to borrow her clothes. Even the designer ones were sexier than anything my mother would let me buy. I remember her looking at me in one of her tight black dresses.

"It's yours honey," she said. "Hell, you fill out the bust better than I do. For my senior prom, I stuffed a dress with balloons. Sure the hell scared that poor boy when he tried to pin a corsage on me."

Millie let us do the things our mom wouldn't—drive her car before we were old enough, wear her make-up, stay up all night if we so chose, have one of her special alcoholic drinks, watch any movie or television show, parade around the house in her high heels, read her juicy novels. At Millie's house, the only rule was "anything goes."

The mood in the room changed in more ways than one when she entered it. If you were in her inner circle she would do anything in the world for you, but if you crossed her, you would immediately feel her rage.

She always had a story or a great comment that accompanied her full belly-laugh. Food was another way Millie helped you solve problems. I can still taste that creamy rich cherry cheese cake Millie made. Her shelves were loaded with gourmet cook books, and she tried making everything, especially marinated French dishes. While she watched her own weight, she would give the rest of us a pinch and a plate of food with the comment, "Look at you, you're too thin. It isn't healthy." One could have weighed 300 pounds, and she would still give you the same line. How could you not love someone who always told you that you were too thin?

When her own kids were grown and she was widowed, she traveled around the world and had men friends. But when asked why she hadn't married again, she answered, "At this age the damn men are only looking for a nurse or a purse." She was a very independent lady, who at times frustrated her children who tried to help her.

I've been told by family members that a good part of her gaudy outgoing personality was due to her love of alcohol. There may be some truth in this. In her 80s she was kicked out of a nursing home after she solicited a worker with the line, "Sex for a bottle of Jack!" I don't know why they made her leave. I would do the same for chocolate if they took it away from me.

These thoughts were going through my head as I waited for my aunt to come to the lounge of her new nursing home. I wasn't prepared for the emaciated, wheel-chair bound gray-haired old lady in a terry-cloth bathrobe who eyed me cautiously. I thought of her own words of wisdom: "You only wish old age on your enemies."

My cousin, her son, had warned me that my aunt not only had cancer, but that she also had Alzheimer's, and she may not know who I was. So when she looked up and asked me with a twinkle in her eye, "Charrie, what stocks are you buying today?" I felt special like I always did when I was with her. She was still Aunt Millie.

# The Autograph Book

Dreary, wet, and cold; a perfect day to clean a closet, especially one that hasn't been looked into for years.

Alone and dressed in my old jeans and a sweatshirt, I was determined to start getting rid of some of my stuff. I balanced a chair in the closet and reached high up on the top shelf—a good place to start.

I grabbed hold of an old, heavy cardboard box. Holding it in one hand and the side of the chair in my other hand, I barely made it down to the closet floor without falling.

Moving the box to the bed, I remembered taking it from my mother's house after she died, and I vaguely recalled it having papers of mine she had kept.

Upon opening it, I pulled out a group of drawings and school papers carefully signed in the handwriting of a young child. I figured they would be fun to show to my grandchildren, but that thought lasted for just a short time, as I remembered how my son and his kids barely looked at his old school papers when I brought them to his house.

A realization we all must come to some time in our lives is: Unless they are collectibles worth money, our treasures are important only to us. So I put the papers in the recycle bin.

Then, I returned to the box to see what other treasures I had kept through my grade school years. There was a small, furry stuffed dog, a silver charm bracelet, and a blue zippered booklet.

The booklet intrigued me. It was approximately five inches square, and on the cover were the words "Class of '56, O'Keefe, Charlene Packer."

In my hand was my grammar school autograph book, At O'Keefe School, the last month before graduation was spent making sure that everyone in your class signed your book. My class had 63 members, thirteen- and fourteen-year-olds all, so I sat back in the bed preparing for a long reading.

Turning the pages, I discovered that, unlike in my high school yearbook, classmates at age thirteen or fourteen didn't have much to say. Most of my friends either wrote something like "Best of luck in high school," "Hope to see you at Hyde Park High," or a "Roses are red; violets are blue" type of rhyme. There weren't many original thoughts in the book, so I concentrated on picturing the kids. It had been 56 years since I thought about many of them, so I discovered I had forgotten a good many. Unlike my high school and college, my grammar school never had a reunion, nor did one tend to hold on to friends from such a young age.

Of the ones I remembered, some of the names brought back fond memories, and others made me chuckle as I thought about how differently they had turned out compared to their young personalities. There was Steve, the troublemaker who became a policeman; Stuart the smartest and handsomest boy in class who became a famous lawyer, only to end up in jail; and Ronnie, the class dummy who became a multimillionaire.

The first page of my book was signed by Michael, with the following verse: "Ha-Ha, again I made it to the first page before anyone else." A lump developed in my throat when I thought about Michael. He loved to be the first to do anything, and he had been the first in our class to die. He was in his sophomore year of high school when he collapsed on the basketball court and was gone. As 14-year-olds we were shocked and surprised, but naïve enough to put it out of our minds and carry on with our lives. The lump developed in my throat because having lost a child of my own, I realized how devastating Michael's death was to his family.

I kept turning the pages trying to picture or remember the names of the signers until I stopped cold at the page signed by Leah. She wasn't in my grammar school; she went to a private girls' school, but we were in the same religious school class for a year.

Leah was a very pretty little girl with long straight black hair and a devilish smile that exposed a dimple on her right side. She was very popular with the boys and girls in our religious school class, but not with the teachers. In the 1950s, girls didn't talk back or act independent. Girls were sweet obedient creatures. This was not Leah's nature, and I tended to watch her antics from a distance until the day I arrived at religious school very early and sat down on a swing in the playground.

Shortly thereafter, Leah joined me. It was a beautiful spring day so when Leah suggested we take a walk to the drugstore down the street I decided to join her. We ordered sodas and talked and talked. When I started to go towards school, she convinced me to ditch and stay with her.

When Leah ordered me to not tell my mother, she doomed an obedient little 13-year-old to a lifetime of guilt. As soon as I read what she wrote in my autograph book I knew 13-year-old Leah had given me that order to test and tease me.

*Charlene was the girl from Havana*
*She slipped on a peel of banana*
*She wanted to swear*
*But her mother was there*
*So she whistled the Star Spangled Banner*

# Battleground: Leftovers

*"The most remarkable thing about my mother is that for 30 years she served the family nothing but leftovers. The original meal has never been found."*
—Calvin Trillin

In a restaurant, if I turned to talk with the friends we were dining with or went to the ladies' room, my plate of food would disappear.

No, it wasn't that the waiters were so efficient. It was my husband, Sam, who was packing up our half-eaten orders to make sure we had leftovers at home.

Sam came from a family in which plates were cleaned and no food was ever thrown out. I came from a family in which it was good manners to leave something on your plate, and leftovers were sometimes eaten the next day, but just as often thrown out. Our differences concerning leftovers were not as troubling when there were two growing boys and a dog in the family. But now that we are retired empty nesters, leftovers have become a battleground.

I could be happy that Sam's attitude minimizes my need to cook. If I make a meal from scratch one day a week and we eat out two, Sam can stretch the leftovers to cover our meals for the rest of the week, or even more. Although I may be required to make the leftover chicken into a pot pie, the leftover beef into chop suey, or the bread that is about to turn green into French toast.

I can handle converting leftovers into another meal, but I can't handle watching them turn moldy. I've tried to tell Sam that the cat ate the food, but that line doesn't work the way it did when we had dogs. That darn cat won't touch any people food but tuna, and Sam knows it.

Many mornings are spent with Sam asking, "Did you throw out my…?" Usually, I actually didn't. It is just that the refrigerator is so packed with Styrofoam or aluminum foil containers that he can't find what he is looking for. Then, once every two weeks, I brace myself for a fight and clean out the refrigerator in anticipation of new leftovers.

There must be a leftover gene. On the day of my marriage, my mother-in-law was busy packing wedding food into her shopping bag; the refrigerator at my son Mike's house is full of Styrofoam and aluminum foil containers.

"After 45 years I guess I can't change Sam," I said to myself recently as I munched on week-old chocolate cake.

I don't consider chocolate in the leftover category.

# Elephants In The Room

Aunt Rose was 92, and had been physically and mentally ill for a long time. We anticipated her death, so when it came there was some relief. At least she wasn't suffering any more. She had been the one who always said, "You wish old age on your enemies"—and she was the one who out-lived her brothers and sister by at least by ten years.

As I boarded the plane for the trip to a small town somewhere near Syracuse, NY, where my aunt would be buried, it occurred to me that I was now the matriarch of the family—the oldest cousin, the one at the top of the pyramid. However, no one in my family died in the order of birth. Some lived to their 90s; some, like my mother, died in their early 50s.

I had used miles and treated myself to first class, so when the flight attendant offered me a glass of wine, I was happy to accept it. I sipped the merlot slowly as I wondered who would show up at the funeral. There were five cousins, the children of my aunt's three brothers and one sister.

Five cousins who had once lived in Chicago within blocks of each other, and who now were scattered across the country. Five cousins who were no longer children. The youngest was 55; the eldest—me—was 68. All the cousins had not been together since Uncle Danny died some 15 years ago. Oh, it's easy to miss weddings, bar mitzvahs, and birthdays, but not funerals. Families are very important to funerals. Only with families can you share a complete history, and thus achieve closure.

My cousin Maureen picked me up at the airport. I hardly recognized her. What really threw me was the color of her hair. It was now short and gray, instead of those long black curls she once had, and she was dressed in overalls and a plaid shirt with no makeup. She did look healthy and fit. We greeted each other with a hug.

As we walked towards the car, she said, "I told you to be casual. This isn't Chicago." I guess she didn't like my obligatory black funeral dress, high heels, and fox fur-collared coat. This comment came from a girl whose mother was the most glamorous person I had ever met. Aunt Rose, Maureen's mother, in her day only wore expensive, stunning clothes; perfect makeup; and matching purses, shoes, and jewelry one could die for. I remembered when Maureen tried in vain to live up to her mother's quest for class and style. My mental reaction to Maureen's comment was, "Hey, cousin, we've traveled different paths in life."

Instead of starting off on a bad foot I turned my attention to the scenery. I soon understood what she was saying, as we passed farm after farm without seeing anything with which a city girl would be familiar. Miles of crops, corn as high as an elephant's eye, and large black-and white cows grazing in lush green fields were in my sight.

Before pulling into her acreage, which was a massive piece of flat-to-hilly land bordered by mature oak trees, I asked, "Where do you shop?"

"There is a shopping center about ten miles down," she answered. Without commenting that I thought "ten miles down" wasn't exactly close, I turned back to the scenery. Soon she turned right up a hilly gravel driveway. In my immediate view was her ranch-style wooden house, plus several white barns, or some sort of farm-type buildings, anyway. I knew my cousin lived on a farm, but my city-girl mentality really didn't get it until now.

I turned to Maureen and said, "I did bring a pair of blue jeans."

"Good," she answered, with the dimpled smile I remembered.

We exited the van and moved through a wire-gated area where multi-colored chickens clucked and grazed. Maureen turned towards me and said, "Be careful where you step. We've had a season of torrential rain and overflowing creeks. Many of the areas are still muddy."

I stepped carefully around the chickens and the wet grass in an effort to keep from ruining my expensive shoes, while thinking, "I never knew chickens came in so many different colors."

I said to Maureen, "I thought you raised horses, not chickens."

"It's a 30-acre farm we're on," she replied. "Just raising horses got boring, so we added chickens."

"For the eggs?" I asked carefully.

As we entered the back door of the house, Maureen gave me her dimpled smile again and said, "Yes, just for the eggs."

I gave out a sigh of relief. I had to ask, just in case she was serving chicken for dinner. My mind wandered back to the old butcher shops on the South Side of Chicago with the sawdust floors, squawking chickens waiting to be killed, and the raw, acid smell of their blood. I shook my head at the thought, and followed Maureen into the house.

Milling around Maureen's country kitchen with the dark wood cabinets and blue-and-pink flowered wallpaper were cousins Billy and Barbara; Maureen's husband, Mark; and Billy's wife, Jesse. We hugged, kissed, and greeted each other like family does, inquiring about our trip here and our children and grandchildren.

Somebody called me "Di," and he name struck me funny. Nobody had called me Di in decades, not even my late husband or my daughter. It was a name from my childhood. I was Diane, or Dr. Wood to everyone else.

Billy, who had been the handsomest young man in the neighborhood, tall and slim with a full head of black curly hair, was now obese and bald. But I kept my mouth shut. I knew he had many medical problems, and he was the only boy out of the five of us.

Barbara gave me a wink, while she patted the chair next to her, beckoning me to join her. She was only a year younger than I was and, even though she lived in California, we managed to keep in close touch through the years. Her job brought her to Chicago often.

I threw my heels off, hid my Gucci purse behind a chair, and sat down next to Barbara at the heavy oak table, with Aunt Rose's out-of-place crystal chandelier hanging above us.

Inhaling the pungent smell of garlic in the soup in front of Barbara, I raised my spoon and asked, "May I taste your soup?"

Billy shook his head in dismay, saying, "Garlic and cheesecake for dinner!"

Barbara rubbed her arms and shivered. She called out, "Maureen, it's cold in here. Do you have a sweater?"

Maureen returned with a homemade knit blue-and-maroon sweater with a big crocheted flower on the front. "Your blood has thinned out since you moved to California," Maureen said. "It's forty degrees outside and at least sixty-five in here."

I picked up the sweater, and admired my aunt's talent. "How I wish I could make something like this," I said.

"You've been saying that for years—long before you started to shake," Maureen said. "No way, now. Want to tell us what is going on?"

"One elephant out of the room," I replied. "Possibly Parkinson's, but I don't want to talk about it now."

There were no questions or comments. My wishes were respected, probably because everyone was thinking about Uncle Max's devastating battle with the disease. I got up and took a bathroom break.

Surprisingly, no children and only one spouse besides Mark were present.

Barbara and I were husband-less. Mine had died eight years ago, and Barbara was between numbers two and three, or was it three and four? I was never sure.

Whenever I was asked why I hadn't married again, I would quote Aunt Rose: "At my age the men are only looking for a nurse or a purse." I had one son, and Barbara had a ton of kids and grandkids, all with different last names.

I turned to Billy, who was on his second or third plate of food. "Is your sister coming?" I asked.

"I think so," he said. "You know how Suzanne is, busy all the time promoting her books."

We had a celebrity in the family, a famous author who appeared on television talk shows and sold thousands of novels, and had tons of money, which was lucky for her, because clearly none of us had an enormous inheritance. All our parents either died with little money left or they had become dependent on us.

We sat around Aunt Rose's dining room table eating on her pink, blue, and yellow-flowered hand-painted Limoges dishes, telling each other how wonderful our lives were. The doorbell rang and Suzanne breezed in as a famous person would, with a driver from New York City carrying her luggage. Nice beige Tumi case, big enough for a week's stay. We were now complete.

Suzanne was the spitting image of her mother—small cute nose, large deep-set brown eyes, and long shapely legs. But her disposition was more dramatic than Aunt Lily's. When we were all youngsters, Suzanne wrote and staged plays for us cousins to perform for the family. She had a unique imagination, probably because she was such a prolific reader. Now she had turned her stories into books and movies. We were very proud of her.

Suzanne handed Maureen a bottle of expensive champagne, only to be told by Mark, "We don't allow alcohol in our home, and we don't celebrate funerals."

Things then became a little strained until Maureen brought out the old picture albums, with many black-and-white photographs. Suddenly, we were all young again, laughing, and crying as the stories flowed. The only thing that betrayed us was the sudden appearance of several pairs of reading glasses.

The spirit of all the absent family members joined us through those pictures.

So many of the pictures brought back memories of those holiday dinners, where 25-to-30 people were stuffed into our small apartments, everyone brought a favorite dish of food and participated in the cleaning and serving, we all talked at once, and the pitch of the conversations kept rising.

A flood of aromas, sweet and sour, from boiling chicken soup to home-made bread, to the sound of voices, to the banging of pots and pans, and to the barking of dogs all came back to me. As in yesteryear, the present-day conversation came fast, too.

"Remember when Uncle Max and Uncle Danny almost had a fist fight over some political issue?"

"It couldn't have been a political issue. In those days in Chicago, we were all Democrats and agreed with whatever the bosses told us."

"So what else is new? Anyway, when grandma said, 'Ganug' (enough), they stopped like it never happened."

"Nobody fought with grandma. She was the matriarch."

I stood up. Poking my chest, I proclaimed, "Hear, hear, I am now the oldest. You must listen to me!" I was totally ignored.

"Does anyone have the recipe for the apple kugel? I loved that, and have never been able to duplicate it."

"What about grandma's poppy seed cookies? I have a recipe but they never come out right."

"Oh, that is because she told us to put in two teaspoons of baking soda, when you really need two teaspoons of baking powder."

"That does make a difference."

"Remember the year my dog Scooter jumped up on the table and ran off with the brisket?"

We all burst into laughter, as we pictured grandma and her daughters, our mothers, running after the dog.

Barbara popped a chocolate-covered strawberry into her mouth, saying "Who brought these? They are sinful, and I need to lose weight for my granddaughter's bat mitzvah. She looked up and smiled. It will be a happy occasion where we can all gather again. Remember May 14."

We shook our heads in an affirmative gesture, though we knew most of us would not travel to Israel to join the celebration. And with the number of intermarriages in the family there won't be many other bar mitzvahs.

Funny, a funeral is different. Everyone shows up to bury family. My immediate family can claim the largest funeral of all. Everyone showed up when my eight-year-old brother was run over by a car, but nobody ever talked about it, or why my father was in the hospital with the bars on the windows for two years. It's now over sixty years later, and I still don't know what happened. Anyway, I was only four, and I hardly remember my brother; not like my mother, who never forgot him.

As the new matriarch of the family, I could identify people in the pictures unknown to the others, and tell a few secrets that only the oldest was privileged to know.

Barbara held up a picture and asked, "Who is that blonde sitting next to Uncle Manny?"

"My dad's secretary," answered Suzanne.

"His secretary—and his girlfriend," I smugly interrupted, putting down my coffee cup, while I reached across the table for one of Maureen's home-made chocolate brownies.

"Really!" the chorus from the table echoed.

"No wonder my mother was always on vacation somewhere," Suzanne said. "His secretary was at all our parties. I liked her, because she always brought us gifts. Jesus, what was her name? She had a funny name." Suzanne knit her eyebrows and looked down in thought. "I wonder why my parents didn't divorce?" she seemed to ask herself.

"I think her name was Tillie," Barbara said. "I remember she had this tiny voice, barely above a whisper." As if she had read Suzanne's mind, Barbara added, "Anyway, divorce in the 'fifties was a dirty word."

"Not like today, huh Barb? What husband are you on now, three, four, five?" Billy volunteered with a smirk.

Suzanne looked at her brother, whose eyes were flaring and whose face now had a petulant look, and decided to change the subject before things got ugly.

I took a bathroom break. I lingered in the bathroom taking in the familiar 1960s colors: the pink tiles, the pink flowered cotton curtains, and the white poodle-knit Kleenex box cover.

Holding my hairbrush in mid-air, I stared at the woman in the small, pink wood-framed mirror. She was much different from the young girl in Maureen's pictures. It wasn't just the gray hair, but the hair's thinness and shortness. The soft face on the girl with the bright happy smile had now become a hard, sad look. Life experiences had left their mark. I took a deep breath, returned the smile to my face, and went back into the dining room to join my cousins.

"Di, remember the walkie-talkies we had from our window on the third floor to your window on the second floor?" Suzanne asked. "How primitive compared to today's cell phones and digital devices, but what fun we had with them."

Still angry with Billy, I gave an uncalled-for response. "What I remember the most about living below your family in the same building was the fights. Your mom and dad would be screaming at each other and that awful dog would be barking continuously."

Billy ignored my comment about his parents' fights, and said, "You have to hand it to my dog Scooter: every time he ran away from home, or my dad let him out on purpose, he found his way back."

Maureen giggled, "Remember when a police car showed up and we all scattered with fear, watching from the sidelines as Scooter emerged strutting alongside the policeman who was returning him home?"

We all laughed until Suzanne quietly said, "I remember another police car showing up to escort my father to the station after he broke my mother's nose."

We looked at each other with surprise. Nobody but Suzanne remembered that.

She continued, "My father was an alcoholic, but in those days it was kept hush-hush. I was an alcoholic too, but I have been sober for two years. Did anyone read my last book? It really isn't fiction."

We were silent for a few moments, in shock over her statement, until

Barbara stood up and said, "We are all proud of you Suzanne." Then one by one, we hugged her.

Maureen walked around the table with hot coffee, as no one was in a hurry to leave soon. I lingered over one photo of a large family gathering around a big dining room table. It was an old one, because we were young and even my grandmother was still alive. What really caught my eye was the money on the table. "What were we doing?" I asked.

Barbara answered, "We were playing poker. Grandma loved to gamble. See the money and the cards at the end of the table?"

"Oh, yes," I answered. "So when Uncle Max moved with the traveling crap game, the gene came from his mother? No wonder my husband banned me from Vegas."

I said this without revealing how much I had managed to gamble away in my early days. Barbara and I exchanged glances. A private understanding had existed between us for years.

"Who is on my mom's lap?" Suzanne asked.

"Judging by the pony tail, I think it's me," Barb said, while resting her chin in the palm of her hand.

"No, you would have been older, and your hair was never that dark," I replied. "I would say Maureen."

We put that picture back on the table and went on to another, still not sure who was on grandma's lap.

Maureen returned from the kitchen with a large plate of cookies. She passed it around the table. "Please eat them," she said. "I don't want to be tempted."

Barbara yelled across the table, "Maureen we need more coffee, and please make it stronger."

Maureen started to go back to the kitchen when Mark appeared and took the coffee pot out of her hands. "I'll take care of it."

I watched him walk back to the kitchen. He was the strong, silent type. Still looking good at fifty-seven, broad shoulders, narrow bottom, with a working man's rugged hands. I wondered if he was always as helpful as he had been today, or if it was a show for the cousins.

"Who has all the antiques in grandma's china cabinet?" Suzanne asked, as she pointed to the cabinet in one of the old pictures. It was a beautiful large mahogany breakfront with beveled glass. Cut glass, majolica, china plates, and an assortment of good and mediocre tchotchkes were overflowing through the lighted wooden shelves.

Maureen answered, "Most are boxed in my basement. My mom, being the oldest and the last survivor, kept them. We can go through the boxes tomorrow. They really aren't worth much. There are boxes of letters too."

Maureen turned towards me, and said, "You may want to read some of them. They could unravel some of our family secrets. Did you know Uncle Max was gay?"

I was in shock from that statement. He was my favorite uncle.

"Why would you say that?" I demanded. "Just because he never married doesn't make him gay."

"He wrote my mother a letter back in the 'thirties when he was in college," Maureen replied.

"In those days he would have had to have been discreet," Barbara added. "He couldn't have come out of the closet."

Before I could ask Maureen what the letter said, her husband called her outside to help him with the horses.

"I would like some of the antiques for the memories," Suzanne said. "Do you have the statue of Centurion? I recently read that Cinderella's original name was Centurion. My mother and grandmother thought the statue was just of a gypsy girl. It would go well with my new book, about peasants."

Billy shook his head as he got up from the table. "Stop talking already, Suzanne," he said. "Haven't you noticed Maureen left the room?"

I picked up a picture of my beloved Uncle Max. Billy leaned in to look at it. "She's right you know," Billy said. "He was always dressed to the hilt, and he did have a lot of men friends!"

"Stop it Billy," I shouted as I raised my hand and swung at him. He pulled back, and I missed him.

"Ha ha," he sang out. Just like the days of yore.

Uncle Max was the only one I could talk to about my brother. He used to say my mom was lucky to have an heir and a spare, and now that she was down to the spare I better take very good care of myself.

Rising from my chair I followed Maureen out the back door, almost bumping into Jesse as she emerged from a nap in the master bedroom.

"How is your headache?" I asked, thinking being married to Billy would give anyone a perpetual headache.

By the time she answered I was half way out the door, walking across the wet green grass, following Maureen and Mark's voices until I found myself at the door of the barn housing the horses. From the corner of the barn I watched the two of them tenderly caring for a foal. In that moment I understood why they had given up comfortable city jobs and moved to a farm. After spending time and money trying to have children they had decided to make farm animals their children.

I backed away and hurried down the path to the house. A cold breeze passed across my skin. I lowered my head and tucked my hands in my pockets, wondering why I had run out without my coat.

"Jesse, it's late, let's go," Billy yelled, as he took his coat from the front closet.

We watched him limp out the door, with his wife dutifully following. Jesse, a quiet shy soul, seemed to respond only to Billy's voice.

I turned to Suzanne, and asked, "Is Billy okay? He looks awful."

Suzanne looked around to make sure Billy and his wife were safely out of range. Her face tightened, "He has diabetes, won't watch his weight, and his business is failing, but he won't let me help," she said. "He has always been stubborn and arrogant."

I made a mental note to contact him when I got back. Billy might take help from me faster than from his sister. I got up and walked over to the picture window facing west, and gazed at the radiant orange glow of the sun slowly setting across the azure sky and cool green hills. A calmness engulfed me.

Back in the dining room, I watched Suzanne biting her nails; Barbara sitting on one foot, drinking her unending cup of coffee; Maureen scurrying back in the house, busy clearing the table, unable to sit still for more than a few minutes; and me analyzing everyone—all habits we've taken with us from childhood.

We could laugh over the stories from the past now. Somehow, with the years, the tragedies did not seem that terrible, maybe because we were older and had learned that though life can break your heart and wound you, it also can provide joy and happiness, and most of all you can survive.

The phone call came just as we were putting on our coats and calling it a day. The shocked look on Maureen's face made us stop in fear and anticipation.

"Billy's been in a car accident. The paramedics have taken him to Belleview Hospital."

Everyone started talking at once as Mark shuffled us into his van, and raced across the bumpy, foggy, country road.

"My baby brother, oh God, don't take him," Suzanne cried. "I promise to be better to him." Suzanne's lips quivered and tears streamed down her face.

"We were kind of mean to him, weren't we?" Barbara whispered.

"Not really," I answered. "We babied him as the only boy, and teased him always. He would have been surprised if we were different now."

"He'll be all right, I know it," Maureen said.

"He has nine lives," I said. "Remember when he hid in the dryer, and Aunt Lily started to turn it on?"

"That was our fault," Suzanne responded. "We wanted him to stop bothering us, and we told him to go hide. We never planned to look for him. God, that kid would do anything for attention."

"I guess it was tough being the baby and only boy among the cousins," Barbara said.

"What about the time he got hit by a baseball, and it took him a few minutes to regain consciousness?" Maureen recalled. Billy had been a muscular teen, hitting that baseball across the fence more than the other boys did.

"That was in his teen years," Suzanne said. "You forgot when he threw a ball at the movie screen at the Hamilton Theatre. He was angry because the projector stopped working."

"The owner of the theater, Mr. Manuskin, pulled down his pants and spanked him," Barbara said. "Today Manuskin would be in jail for child abuse!"

"Back then no one would hesitate to discipline any child who needed it," I said.

"So true; back in the 'fifties it was hard to get away with anything," Suzanne replied. "There were ears and eyes everywhere."

Barbara shuffled through her purse, desperately looking for something.

My eyes met hers. I shook my head and whispered, "Not here. You can hold out."

My cousin was addicted to Valium, and I was the one who had first had it recommended it for her.

Mark interrupted us with, "What about his wife, Jesse. Is she hurt?"

Ashamed, Suzanne, Barbara, and I looked at Maureen for an answer. Billy was blood, and the one we worried the most about, even though Jesse had been around over twenty years.

Maureen gazed at her husband, and sucked in her breath before answering, "She was the one who called, so I assume she is fine."

Mark just kept driving, getting us there in a little less than twenty-five minutes.

Belleview Hospital was small by my standards, but neat and immaculate, nothing like the city hospitals. The four cousins attacked the triage nurse sitting at the emergency room registration desk with a barrage of questions and demands. She eyed us with disdain until she recognized Maureen.

"Maureen, please control your friends," the nurse said.

Maureen moved up to the desk. "Sorry Jane, but my cousins and I are very anxious. Our cousin Bill Greenwald was brought in after a car accident."

Suzanne stepped forward, and said "He's my brother, and I demand…"

Maureen gave her a dirty look as the nurse busied herself with some papers.

"He's in Room 12 and we can only allow one," Nurse Jane said. As the four women pushed forward, Jane gave up and said, "Please be quiet. There are other patients, too."

Mark stayed in the waiting room, which was practically empty. He sat down on one of the perfectly aligned green padded chairs, happy to be away from the women.

The four of us raced to Room 12 in time to see an orderly wheeling Billy out to the hall, while Jesse stood in the doorway.

I broke in front of everyone. "I'm Dr. Wood," I said. "Where are you taking him?"

Billy raised his head, and gave me a disgusted look. "Doctor, my eye," he said. "You have a PhD in psychology. What are you trying to pull?"

"At least your personality hasn't changed," I responded. "What happened?"

"I'm going for X-rays," Billy said. "They think my leg is broken. Otherwise I'm fine."

Suzanne moved forward and gave her brother a big hug, while the orderly quietly said, "They are waiting for him in X-ray."

As they wheeled Billy away, he said, "Damn it, you got me all wet."

Suzanne smiled as she wiped the tears from her mascara-marked face.

I watched them wheel him off, thinking of the little boy who fell off the swing while I was flirting with cool Jeff Blazer instead of watching him. I felt guilty for the six weeks four-year-old Billy had his arm in a cast.

The six of us waited for him to come out of the emergency room with his modern-day cast before calling it a day. We quietly emptied the coffeepot while Nurse Jane kept an eye on us.

I walked over to Jesse, and asked, "How did the accident happen?"

"There was a slow drizzle, making it hard to see down the dark, unfamiliar roads," Jesse replied. "Suddenly a teenage kid on a bicycle appeared right in front of our car. Billy swerved to keep from hitting him, and he ended hitting a car coming from the other direction."

My mind flashed back to that day so many years ago when a big black car with fins pulled out of our garage and hit my brother on his bicycle. I've never been able to go beyond that image, and no one in the family would ever talk about it. To this day I have no idea who was driving that car. I need to check out those old letters Maureen has. They may finally bring out another elephant from the closet.

Tomorrow we will bury the last survivor of one generation. Now it was up to the next generation, the five cousins, to keep the family together. Because family is important.

They are the keepers of the elephants!

# The Gates Are About to Close

I pace back and forth, sure that the gates will close and we will miss our plane. As the other passengers board I am nervously waiting for my sister to come back with her cup of Starbucks.

Of course we don't miss the plane. As usual, she manages to make it just before the doors close. She smiles at me. "Oh, they're boarding already," she comments. I don't have to answer because the flight attendant announces, "The gates are about to close" as we scramble onto the plane.

After we settle comfortably in our seats, she turns to me and says, "You and dad would be the first ones in line at the concentration camps."

She hit the nail on the head; our differences in personality go way back. I am like my father—always early, doing everything yesterday; and she is like my mother—always late, doing everything tomorrow. Both equally annoying habits.

We arrive at the Detroit airport, gate ten, and scurry down the concourse to gate 59. I'm in a panic; we have only 40 minutes before our connecting plane takes off. Somewhere around gate 40 she decides we have time to stop for lunch. I'm nervously tapping my fingers while we wait for the lunch to arrive.

When our sandwiches finally get to the table I pay the bill and make my sister leave with sandwich in hand. "What a dumb idea to stop for lunch," I say to her. "We have only ten minutes before the flight boards."

I run her down the concourse to gate 59, anticipating a closed gate.

Of course I'm wrong. The plane is not even there yet. A 20-minute delay is posted.

She gives me a dirty look as she walks off to get another cup of coffee. I just slink into a chair and wait.

We make it on the plane and to our destination with only one other mishap. She almost left her suitcase in the airport. But as usual, everything worked out for her. It always does, although I don't know why.

To her credit, she is a very efficient designer working two jobs, while I am retired, with less pressure. On the other hand, she has set a pattern whereby everyone expects her to be late, and would be shocked if she wasn't. And her last-minute-itis has been passed down to the next generation. I've heard her son say, "Mom, we have ten minutes. Do you want to go see a movie?"

I guess it goes back to when she was a three year-old stage performer singing, "I'm a slow poke now."

I guess nobody told her that it wasn't supposed to be a lifetime project!

# Heaven or Hell?

We originally thought of meeting where our friendship began. Someplace near Hyde Park High School in Chicago—but we abandoned that idea when we heard President Obama was in town. Visiting the neighborhood near his home would be impossible.

We both now lived in the northern suburbs of Chicago, so we chose a place called Phil's in the suburb of Lincolnshire, which was halfway between us.

I thought about how pleasant the warm spring afternoon was as I pulled into the restaurant's parking lot. And Phil's was one of my favorite eating places, because it was located in a converted old "painted lady" mansion. The wooden porch surrounded most of the building and featured an enormous old swing. I breathed in the aroma of the beautiful lilies, gardenias, and multiple flower beds surrounding the three wooden steps leading to the stained glass door.

Inside the rooms were decorated with blue flowered wallpaper, converted old gas chandeliers, and china knick-knacks. I requested one of the tables tucked into a tranquil side room, and sat down at a table with a white tablecloth and a wooden captain's chair.

The waitress, a plump blond girl with a dimple on her right cheek, approached with a menu. I smiled and said, "I'm waiting for another person."

"Something to drink while you are waiting?" she asked.

"Black coffee," I answered

She returned with a pot of coffee and a basket of warm rolls.

True to my nature, I was there at least twenty minutes early, so I poured myself a cup of coffee and opened the newspaper I had brought. After perusing the news of who had shot whom, an unusual story caught my eye. It was about a woman who had a near-death experience, and witnessed the usual beautiful lights and celestial angels. A bizarre thought crossed my mind. I've never read about someone in a near-death experience who said, "The Devil met me and dragged me to the brink of Hell before I suddenly woke up."

Even to the end we must not hang out the dirty laundry. We all lived in "the best of times," and we all went to Heaven in the end.

I related this to my lunch today. Through the Internet I've reconnected with a high school friend, one I hadn't seen in more than fifty years, even though we both still lived in Illinois. She was one of those friends whom I could bare my soul to, whom I shared my teenage crushes and heartaches with, knowing they would be kept just between the two of us. She moved in and out of my house like a family member, calling my mother "Mom," too. She was a friend with a capital F.

I wondered about when we finally met up today, after the first half hour of reminiscing and updating on whom we kept in touch with and what happened in their lives, what will we talk about?

Will it be only the heavenly things in our lives, or will we feel that old connection that will allow us to bare our souls? Will we just state good facts or will we be able to admit that once in a while the Devil invaded our lives too?

I poured another cup of coffee and reached for one of those warm rolls while I pondered whether I was reading too much into a teenage friendship. Maybe we were just kids clinging to the same problems, crushes and dreams that my teenage grandchildren are experiencing now. Maybe we were not unique, just young.

My logical mind knew the five-foot-four, 100-pound teenager with an hour-glass figure, long coal-black hair, and unending energy wasn't going to walk through the restaurant's door, but that was the person I still was looking for.

A shiver ran down my spine as I watched a mature woman wearing a long, flowered dress, adorned with multiple gold chains, enter through the restaurant door, stop at the receptionist's counter, and then walk towards my table. I immediately recognized her large expressive dark eyes with the thick natural black eyebrows. Her coal-black hair obviously dyed made her look even more familiar than I probably looked with my natural gray locks and plump frame. As my mind took refuge in the 1950s I stood up to greet Diane. We smiled, laughed, and hugged each other.

After the pleasantries and reminiscences, we eventually started talking about the hells we had gone through in our lives. We found ourselves in parallel time universes—talking about the last 60 years, but feeling as comfortable with each other as we had when we were teenagers with our whole lives ahead of us.

And that was truly Heaven.

# The Hoarder Gene

I was outside waiting for Sam to return from the Sunday flea market. When his van pulled up, I eyed his movements carefully. When he opened the back of the van and pulled out a broken-down old bicycle, I snapped.

Marching over to him, I shouted, "That's it! I will not allow another bicycle into my house."

He ignored me. "It's going into the garage," he replied calmly.

"Where in the garage?" I rejoined. "At last count, there were 40 bicycles there, plus all your tools and junk. I haven't been able to put a car in the garage for 35 years."

"Last time you had a garage you drove the car through the wall and into the family room," he replied.

With hands on my hips, eyes narrowed and lips pursed, I answered, "That was our neighbor."

He smiled in his winning way. "Well, if you had a garage you would have copied her," he said sweetly.

I stood there staring as my husband found an inch of space to squeeze another bicycle into our garage.

When I married him more than 45 years ago I didn't realize he was in possession of the bargain-hunting hoarder gene. I should have known when he wrote me from Okinawa that the Army was allowing him to send home 1,200 pounds of stuff.

By the time we got married he had totally furnished our one-bedroom apartment, and after a year we had to buy a bigger place.

I looked to my mother for support when he brought in that first antique dental chair, plunking it down in my front room, but she was no help. She was a product of the Great Depression, and her comments were, "He is a good man. He doesn't drink, he doesn't gamble, and he brings home his money. So what if he likes to shop?"

Little did she know what she was condoning.

I am a product of the 1950s, a time before the women's movement, an era in which the man still had control of the household. Unlike my mother I have a college education and a teaching degree and I can drive, which means I can make some money, but not as much as my dentist husband. However, I can get away if the argument becomes heated.

Bicycles in the garage are a small part of my problem. We have so much stuff that when we retired we had to upgrade to a house twice the size of our other one. For the first year I thought "Isn't this great? We have so much room now." I hadn't realized that a retired shopper and hoarder has twice as much time as he did before.

My friends thought that when my dentist husband established several antique dental office displays throughout the country that my house would start to empty out, but I knew better. He just had more room to collect more old stuff—especially when he found eBay!

When you have a lot of stuff you have responsibilities, and "what ifs."

What if you go on vacation and burglars break in?!

What if the cat scratches the antique furniture, or the dog pees on the sofa?!

What if my friend's grandchild breaks my grandmother's majolica plate?! (Notice I don't say *my* grandchild.)

What if you can't play Mah Jongg or go to the spa because company is coming over and you must spend days dusting your stuff?!

What if you have so much stuff that you can't move in the house, and the fire department condemns your place?!

What if you trip over the hundred pairs of shoes lined up in the bedroom and break your foot, and then you can't take care of your stuff?!

What if you have to spend most of the time looking for missing stuff?!

What if you leave the expensive things to one child and not the other?!

I could go on forever, but after living with the same man for more than 45 years, I know I can't change him, and most of all I've realized there are more important things in life than how your house looks—like health, friendship, and love.

To be fair, I have to admit that I have collected stuff also, but *my* stuff is special!

Sam is welcome to defend himself, but I have a lot of witnesses on my side. Anyway I'm the writer in the family—so I always have the last word, and in print, too!

# Loss and Grief

Fullerton, the main street in this Chicago neighborhood, was busy with cars zooming by from both directions. Two young boys, probably around ten years old and dressed in jeans and baseball shirts, crossed the street with no heed to the traffic. I watched as they dared the cars to hit them. The old teacher in me wanted to discipline them, but that part of me no longer functioned.

The burst of leaves on the trees, and the sprouts of yellow, red, white, and pink flowers spoke of life continuing, but not for me.

The sun set across the sky like an angry orange ball, as it did every day of the last four years. The sun and I were angry all the time, but it was our secret. On the outside, we were stoic and beautiful.

I stood in the doorway half in and half out until a passerby tried to enter. Annoyed, the woman asked, "In or out?" Reluctantly I went back into Children's Memorial Hospital, moving slowly down the hall to the elevator.

As I entered I could not help noticing the bald six- or seven-year-old little boy getting off. I swallowed hard, pressing my lips together to keep the tears from flowing down my face. Tears for him; tears for his parents; and tears for me. And a smile, too: a smile for the memory of the times my son Jeff would flip his wig off in elevators and stores to startle people.

I exited the elevator on floor number three, slowly walking down the hall to the last treatment room in the corridor. I didn't need to ask the nurse anything about my son's condition. In the depths of my soul, I knew our four-and-a-half-year battle with leukemia would soon be over, and I would go home alone without my first-born son.

As I approached the room, I could hear my spunky eight-year-old's voice. "Don't, you'll break my back!" he said. "I did not sign for this. I'll sue you!"

At first, a smile crossed my face, as I thought, "That kid of mine will stand up to anyone." Then I realized where we were, and quickly went to the door.

"My son is screaming!" I yelled inside. "What are you doing to him?"

A nurse came out. "He's fine," she said. "We are giving him a spinal tap. It is dramatic the first time, but it is amazing how fast the kids get used to these tests."

Jeff did get used to the spinal taps and to the bone-marrow and blood tests much easier than I did. He was young, only eight; but so was I, only 33. Young mothers can't believe anything could happen to their children, and young kids believe their mothers will take care of them and make things better. The children always have hope, even when things go from bad to worse.

Though his condition did deteriorate, there were teaser months in which he went into remission and we ever-so-cautiously thought about the future. It took four-and-a-half years of treatment, chemo, and radiation, of ups and downs, torture, and false hopes, before we got to September 11, 1981.

Some 20 years later, September 11 would go down in infamy, like December 7 for Pearl Harbor, and November 23 for the assassination of President John F. Kennedy. For me, September 11 will always be the worst day.

*** 

"It's time to call the family," Jean and Barbara, Jeff's two favorite nurses gently told me. I stood a few minutes, while my eyes rested on the unresponsive, emaciated young body clutching a white stuffed monkey attached to a fake banana. His breathing had become increasingly shallow through the night. This body was a silhouette of that of the vibrant, curly-haired bundle of wit and joy I had known.

I was desolate as I made the necessary calls to my immediate family. They needed to say good-by and I desperately needed their help to cope, and to plan a funeral for my 12-year-old.

Why, I don't know, but as I sat in the death room of Children's Memorial Hospital I remembered some six years ago when a neighbor said to me, "There are worse things than losing your mother." I wanted to tell her she was right. Nothing in the world could compare to watching your 12-year-old son die. "Mom," I mouthed, as I looked up at the sky. "Take care of him."

I will always remember that last day of his life, when the immediate family surrounded the bed and said good-by. I clenched my jaw and pursed my lips in an effort to keep tears back until he took his last breath. A high-pitched scream then echoed from my throat as my husband, Sam, led me from the room.

***

I can't even imagine how the parents of the children at Sandy Hook can deal with the deaths of their youngsters. No warning, no chance to say goodbye, and the horror of identifying a beautiful little child who has been blown to bits. How can we make sense of a world that has gone so wrong? Oh my God, where have you gone?

The world mourns with them, but for how long? Only until the next attack; then the Sandy Hook parents too will mourn alone. Soon the elephant will be in the room, and only the parents will see him. "Why the innocent children?" they will ask. "They never harmed anyone. Why?"

And no one else will even want to hear the question.

I know those parents would easily choose to substitute their own deaths for those of their children if they could. The Hebrew language has a word for a parent who has lost a child. It is *shakul,* meaning reversal of the natural order. In the natural order, parents don't bury their children; children bury their parents.

***

I sat on a soft, brightly patterned sofa beside a pink Formica table laden with magazines and newspapers. Even the walls were dazzling with color. I guessed some designer had thought the room should be cheerful, but frankly, the decor unnerved me. Wearing no makeup and dressed in black to match my mood, I accepted the cup of coffee handed to me by an older woman.

"I'm Trish," she said. "Welcome to the mothers' lounge. In here, you can talk and cry all you want. We are all in the same boat."

"Yes, the Titanic," another mother, a very petite redhead, said.

Trish offered me a cigarette. I hesitated. I had tried to stop several times, but now I needed all the help I could muster. I took a deep puff of the Salem cigarette and watched the smoke rise up against the cold window. I did eventually quit for good on July 15, 1978, at 1 p.m., the day Jeff told me I was killing him with my cigarettes.

I now reserve all judgment of other people. I know I can never understand what another is going through, nor will I ever. The mothers in this room came the closest to understanding each other. Unfortunately in the late 1970s, leukemia and childhood cancers had a very poor cure rate, so we were more pessimistic than optimistic.

This room became my hangout while in the hospital. Only other mothers with children battling cancer could really understand. We waited with Nancy with hope for her son Tim when he was the first in the hospital to go through a bone-marrow transplant. We despaired for her, Tim, and our own children when the bone-marrow transplant failed, after he had gone through unbelievable pain.

I paced back and forth with these mothers when one of our children cried in pain from the effects of a chemotherapy treatment, or when a test came back showing a child was out of remission.

\*\*\*

My husband, my other son, my girlfriends, and my father all tried to get me out of bed and into the real world, a place I couldn't handle after the day that took my child, my faith, and half my mind. I was happy with those wonderful pills that kept my migraines and nightmares at bay by knocking me out.

When I finally got out of bed, I told myself it was for my younger son who needed a mother, but it was really that damn collie puppy who wouldn't take no for an answer. After all, my ten-year-old son went back to school, and my husband back to work, so I had a good part of the day to cry and do nothing. After refusing to answer the phone, and telling friends to leave me alone long enough, most finally did. There were a few who refused to let me turn them away. Those are the ones I still keep around.

I was only 38, but I functioned like an Alzheimer's patient. I went shopping and left the loaded cart in the middle of the aisle, and ran out of the store crying. Too many foods reminded me of my son. I should never have been allowed to drive in those early months. I would stop in the middle of the street and try to remember where I was going. I would get lost on the way to places I'd traveled to for 20 years.

I read books about loss, tossing most of them away. I went to therapy sessions where I just cried. I talked to my rabbi, and still stayed angry with God. I took pills, and either ate too much or starved. I smiled and pretended for my living son, but he knew he had not only lost a brother, but also the mother he had before September 11, 1981. His mother was so afraid that she would lose him, too, that she became emotionally empty and very possessive.

When I finally looked into the mirror, I realized the light had disappeared from my eyes, the smile was no longer there, my back was bent over, and my hair was suddenly tinged with gray. Finally, my best friend made me go to the beauty shop and shopping for clothes, but that just made me feel like a clown—bright and cheerful on the outside, crying on the inside.

My sister and two very close friends who listened without judgment were the ones who kept me going.

*** 

As I was giving blood, the vein collapsed. The nurse apologized as she took the rubber hose off of my left arm. "Let's try your right arm," she said. "Maybe the veins are better there." As she wound the rubber tightly around my arm, I smiled with a knowing grin as she poked me for the second time. I sat very stoic, refusing to flinch—like Jeff.

He was a tough kid. I can hear Jeff's voice, loud and assertive, as he fired a lab tech or a new resident. "You cannot take blood from me," he said. "One try and you are out. Get someone here who knows what he is doing!"

Day after day, week after week, the sharp needles punctured veins on his already black-and-blue arms, hands, and feet. Bright ruby-red blood, smelling like rusty metal, filled the opaque vials.

Once a month bigger needles dug into his spinal column to remove fluid, and into his hip to take bone marrow. They tested and tested. Once in a while he passed the test, and we rejoiced at the word "remission." But it never lasted. Four-and-a-half years of tests, and then the final verdict was a death sentence.

Unlike the parents of the children at Sandy Hook School, we had hope during those years. We ran with the word remission and lived life, doing things we wouldn't have done otherwise. We let Jeff, a boy between the ages of eight and 12, call the shots. He wanted to go to Israel, we went. He wanted to go on the Love Boat, we went. He wanted a motorcycle, he got one. He wanted to ski, he skied. All in between the hospital visits.

We walked through the halls of Children's Memorial dragging the IV pole, carefully avoiding pulling the needle out of his hand.

"Jeff, you should stay in bed," I said. "You had your chemo drip only two hours ago." We are in the hospital getting chemo one week out of every month for the first two years—the standard treatment in the late 1970s.

He stops, and looks at me with that determined look, eyes flaring, and mouth pursed. "I'm going to Julie's birthday party in the playroom," he asserts.

We almost make it when he stops, bends over, and starts to vomit and vomit.

\*\*\*

I tried to go back to the living, to venture into the world away from the family and friends who protected me, but then the inevitable question would come. "How many children do you have?"

If I said "one son," I would be betraying the memory of the son who died. If I said "two," I would have to explain. Sometimes I said, "I lost a child," but that wasn't true. He wasn't lost. I knew where he was—in a hole in the cemetery in Palatine, Illinois. It took me years to not flee from the poor unsuspecting stranger who was just engaging in polite conversation.

My routine was all mixed up. For four-and-a-half years my job was taking care of Jeff. I lived half my life at Children's Memorial; I didn't have time to do anything. Suddenly I had time, more than I ever had before. I had been replaced in my job as a dental office bookkeeper by a computer and two helpers; my younger son had become used to spending time with friends and neighbors; a housekeeper was now helping to clean the house; and the dog had taken my place in the bed sleeping on my pillow vertically next to Sam.

\*\*\*

Clumps of hair are lying on Jeff's pillow every day. Between the radiation and the chemo, he is losing his beautiful thick curly hair. It doesn't seem to bother him, but it wipes me out. Now he really looks like a cancer patient.

Sam is more concerned with the bleeding from Jeff's rectum. Home only two days, and we are back at Children's where again I am sleeping on a chair next to his bed.

\*\*\*

I ran to catch up to the boy. The curly head, the number 34 football shirt— Walter Payton's number. My heart was racing as I overtook the little boy, who was just a short ways ahead of me in the grocery store. "Jeff!" I cried.

The child turned and stared at me, perplexed. "I'm sorry," I whispered as I slithered off. "He's dead, dead, dead, and not coming back," I repeated to myself as I ran out of the store, leaving my full cart in the middle of the aisle.

At home I went into Jeff's room, reached into his drawer, pulled out the number 34 football shirt and became unraveled. His clothes, his toys, and those 50-some stuffed animals stayed in place for many years, like the toys in Eugene Field's poem *Little Boy Blue.*

\*\*\*

It was a routine bone marrow test right at the end of the two-year treatment that threw us out of remission and into the cycle of relapse, remission, and relapse. Instead of going into easy maintenance we went to heavy chemo drugs and more radiation. Jeff's oncologist was almost as disappointed as we were.

Ten-year-old Jeff was angry, not disappointed. He yelled, "I'm done. I'm not getting stuck again." He slammed the door to the doctor's private office and ran. The staff thought he wouldn't go far, but I knew better. While he was being looked for in the hospital, I managed to find him walking down Fullerton Avenue.

We talked about his relapse and treatment. He knew his chances of staying alive were getting slimmer. He asked about Heaven and what it was like to die. Had it been today, he would have looked everything up on the Internet.

Suddenly in the middle of the conversation, he bargained with me, "Buy me a motorcycle, and I will go back to treatment," Jeff said. He got the motorcycle—one that his younger brother would crash into a tree, almost killing himself.

Night after night I lay awake worrying about my son, while I watched my husband sleeping peacefully, lightly snoring. I really wanted to pound him with my fists, screaming "How can you sleep?" but instead I went downstairs to the kitchen followed by the dog, who joined me because he anticipated food was coming. I knew my husband hurt, but he stayed more in control than I did.

The bone pain from the experimental chemo drugs made Jeff's legs useless, and he was now in a wheelchair. The additional radiation gave him unbelievable headaches. Surgery to put in a shunt was the only way to relieve the pain in his head.

I watched from the window of the hospital. The sun glistened against the pane. A ball flew high across the crystal-clear azure sky, before it connected with a large wooden bat. I thought, "That is where my son should be: playing baseball."

When your 12-year-old tells you he no longer wants to live like this, your heart breaks.

My son will never slide behind the wheel of the red Corvette he always wanted, he won't be flirting with teenage girls, nor will he enjoy an orgasm, or walk down the aisle to welcome his bride, or cuddle his own baby son or daughter in his arms.

I hate to admit it, but the only part of the paper I read was the death notices. I was like a person who slows down to look at a car accident—except if the people who died were too old I was angry, and if there was another child listed, I was horrified and guilty.

For many years, I couldn't read any books. I would start and my mind would wander. Then a friend took me to a lecture by Elie Wiesel, and I devoured all his books about the Holocaust. Over and over, I read the part he wrote in *Night* about the child who was hanged.

Dressed in my finest, laughing, joking, sipping wine, and yelling "happy New Year" to my husband and my closest friends felt so good—until the guilt settled in and the tears ran down my face.

"Damn it Char, it's two years. It's time we start living. Don't ruin everyone's good time," my husband told me as he walked me out of the party room.

***

Five days before Jeff died, one of his poems made it into Mike Royko's *Chicago Sun-Times* column. We brought a cake and had a party at the hospital. When I re-read the poem later, I realized how angry Jeff was, even though at the time I just saw a very brave boy who never stopped fighting.

*Life is so unfair*
*One day you are living,*
*The next day you're not*
*So many problems*
*When will they stop?*
*Or will they keep coming until I rot?*
*You gotta fight, fight, fight to stay alive*
*I'm not telling a lie*
*You gotta fight, fight, fight to stay alive.*
Jeffery Wexler, Feb. 8, 1969 – Sept. 11, 1981

***

When did summer end and fall begin? Was it the day the berries fell from the trees and covered the pool, making it almost impossible to enjoy swimming in it, or was it when I needed a sweater for my early walk? The early walk we take every day when the leaves start to turn from smooth emerald green, to bright red and yellow, and then to crunchy dirty brown as they fall off the tree and die.

When did another Labor Day erupt into another September 11? Will it ever get easier?

# No More Free Pie

"Where are you going?" my husband, Sam, asks.

"To have lunch with my sister," I answer.

"You just had lunch with her a few days ago," he says.

I walk out of the house shaking my head. He just doesn't understand. Women need to visit with and talk to other women. We need girlfriends we can trust, ones who love and understand us. Ones who will listen, accept our faults, and are honest with us. Ones who are there for the good and the tragic.

I have several special girlfriends I can count on, but my best friend, the one I've known the longest, and the one with whom I have the most history, is my sister, Bobbi.

We both have busy lives, she more than I, as she still is working while I, the elder, am retired.

In spite of this we make a point of meeting at least once a week.

Bobbi and I live about fifty miles from each other, so we are always looking for a half-way spot. We thought we found a good one at a Baker's Square.

I am always early and Bobbi is always tardy, so on this particular Wednesday afternoon I thought nothing about her being thirty minutes late.

Sitting in a booth towards the middle of the room near the windows, drinking my third cup of coffee, and checking my e-mails on my phone, I was a little alarmed when my bedraggled sister collapsed into the booth, opposite me.

"I'm sorry I'm late but...." This was how most of our meetings began. There was always a good story after the buts, like the time she locked her keys in the car and had to be towed, or when she dropped her cell phone in her coffee cup and she couldn't call me, or when she got delayed in a bakery which had made 12,000 cookies instead of the 6,000 she had ordered for her business demonstrations, or....

Anyway, I cut her conversation off with, "You look a mess. What happened now?"

She answered, "I was on my way when I realized my car was out of gas. Knowing that I was already late, I stopped to get just enough gas to get here. When I pulled the hose out of the pump I spilled gas on me."

Well, she did smell funny. "Are you okay?" I asked. "Do you want to go home and change? You're not going to catch on fire, are you?" I looked around to make sure no one was smoking.

"Don't worry about it," she responded. "I washed off." So I ignored her new dilemma and we proceeded to order lunch and visit.

After about ten minutes we began to notice several employees of the restaurant walking around sniffing and scanning the surroundings in our area. We ignored them and concentrated on our salads and conversation.

Soon, we heard the sounds of fire engines that seemed to be very close—so close, in fact, that firemen actually entered the restaurant and announced over a bullhorn, "Please do not be alarmed, but we suspect a gas leak somewhere towards the middle of the room and we need to evacuate everyone in the restaurant."

Bobbi and I sank down low in our seats while everyone in the restaurant became alarmed and rushed for the exits. Meekly, we approached the firemen.

"I may be the cause of the alarm…" my sister said.

"She spilled gas on herself while pumping it at the station," I said, completing her sentence.

There was no gas leak in the restaurant, of course, and we finished our meal after the chuckling firemen departed, the restaurant staff shooting us dirty looks all the while.

Needless to say, we had to find a new place to meet. Too bad. The pie was so good at Baker's Square, and it was free on Wednesday with a meal.

# Spiritual Connection?

I never believed in psychics, fortune tellers, mediums, mental telepathy, or supernatural beliefs. I enjoy sci-fi books and movies; I think they come from great, imaginative minds. I believe in the theory of evolution, though my inquisitive mind does question what life on Earth is all about, especially as science discovers how vast the Universe is, and how small our little planet is in comparison.

Through the years I've read stories of people who have had out-of-life experiences, or near-death experiences. Nonsense I thought.

I come from a religious upbringing, and never really questioned God until I felt He deserted me in my most precious time of need. While in my early thirties my first born son was stricken with leukemia. For four-and-a-half years I prayed to God to spare him, and to spare all the innocent children in that hospital fighting for their lives.

When my twelve-year-old son died, my faith also died.

I've studied them all: science, religion, art, psychology, and fantasy, and I've come to the conclusion that there is no definite; that the more we know the less we know; and that anything is possible. Things occur in our lives that we have no control over, no matter how calculating we are.

But something happened to me that converted me into being a believer in a possible spiritual being. The event reminded me of the old saying: You never know what someone else experiences until you've walked in their shoes.

One of the wonders of this age is the device I am writing on now. It is called an iPad and it works from some waves in the air called Wi-Fi and the cloud. I can talk to my grandkids two thousand miles away on it. If iPads can talk to each other, I guess there is a possibility that minds can also send signals to each other across miles, and times.

Two months ago I was visiting friends in Florida. Six of us were busy conversing and enjoying a meal prepared in my friend's home. Suddenly I experienced a slight dizzy spell, and everything went black for me. The next thing I remember, five people were around me calling my name.

According to my husband and friends I had suddenly passed out into my plate of food. I was lucky it wasn't hot soup! My husband picked up my head and cleaned off my face, as my friends called my name, and gently poked at me.

I came to with no recollection or lasting effect, except for the phone call I received two hours later. My sister was two thousand miles away from me in a hospital emergency room. At the exact time I passed out she was told she had a brain tumor and six months to live. We are extremely close, and we both believe she called out to me at that time, and I responded to her call.

Now that she has come through a very difficult brain surgery with a good prognosis, contrary to her original one, we both believe not only did we communicate, but somebody up there, like maybe my son, was watching over us.

Since it never hurts to cover all bases, after getting my sister through surgery, I went to my doctor. He checked out the following: I wasn't pregnant (are you kidding?); on alcohol or drugs; wasn't exhausted; didn't have high or low blood pressure; wasn't starving myself (he could have looked at me to answer that one); wasn't choking; and wasn't one who had ever passed out before. After those questions and a complete examination the doctor came up with no real medical reason for me passing out.

There are so many unknowns in this world. The other possibilities could be that I was the one who was dying, and my sister called me back because she needed me; or I really hated the meal; or of course there could be no reason at all.

Does something or someone control which ant we stepped on today? Did Horton really hear a Who? Is it all a matter of spiritual connection?

# The Temperature Games

Thumbing through a magazine, I spotted an article called *Twenty Things To Discuss Before Marriage*. It is a little late for me since my husband and I are close to fifty years of marriage bliss, but from my experienced viewpoint the article left out a major thing to discuss before marriage, and I need to alert you to it.

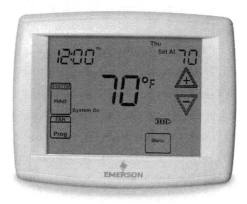

Oh, the article talked about all the regular philosophical things like: How many children do we want? Sorry, you can't decide beforehand. This is an emotional question. What if both of you decide on two and then a night of passion comes along? Suddenly you will have three!

Then there is the subject of money. So easy to discuss money when young and naive, and still in the dream that you can live on love! Just try it.

Religion is always on these lists, especially if the two of you were raised differently. "No brainer," you say—"we will let the kids decide!" Good luck with that one.

Getting along with each other's extended family is another point on the list. I will not go near that one, especially in today's world when there is no longer a family Godfather or Matriarch who ends disputes with, "Because I said so!"

I scrutinized the article carefully, going over topics such as sex, secrets, household duties, and several other items. I had a good laugh over most, but I never did find any talk about the marital subject dear to my heart—temperature!

"Temperature?" you ask. "Is she crazy?" Think about it. Have you ever met a married couple who agreed on the temperature of anything? She is hot, he is cold, she is cold, he is hot, he wants the window open, she is freezing, they both want the blankets, he wants the top down, she wouldn't think of it.

I was taught white can only be worn from Memorial Day to Labor Day. My husband was taught air conditioners can only be used Memorial Day to Labor Day. Doesn't matter if it's 102 degrees the day after Labor Day. Actually, he doesn't even want to use the air conditioner on most summer days anyway, because the heat doesn't bother him.

But the same man who is cold in the summer is hot in the winter. My husband loves drudging through three feet of snow, and keeping the thermometer inside the house around 65 degrees while I sit next to him with my fur coat on, moaning, "Why can't we spend the winter in Florida?"

Temperature problems don't just stay in the house. The car produces temperature conflicts too, especially in autos where the air blows directly on you. I have to dress in my long underwear in the summer to travel a few blocks. Convertibles are where the worst temperature conflicts occur. Top down means wind in the face and the end of a hairdo. Never let your guy buy an auto where the top can go down. You will regret it as you age.

The first 35 years went by and we started to get used to each other and the temperature games we played. Then retirement and an upgrade to a house with a pool came, and so did a renewal of the temperature games. Together 24/7 is tough enough, but now the thermometer gets readjusted hourly.

The summer is the worst. My husband just doesn't think the pool should stay at 90 degrees. I think he only complains because of the high gas and electric bills.

Back to the reason why I wrote this article. I definitely think that temperature should be a major thing to discuss before marriage. In fact I think it should be right up there with love, honor, and obey. So easy to solve. Just pick a number you agree on. I would go for an agreed temperature of 70 degrees! I forgot the pool. I'd need to write in 90 for the pool.

As for me, I plan to ask for separate rooms in the nursing home, though I will miss my husband's warm body next to me in bed. But in my own room I will be able to turn the thermometer up to 75. Game over!

# Thanksgiving in the 21st Century

Fall is in the air, with a slight hint of wintery cold. The trees are bursting with color. The pumpkins, plump and full, are scattered across the fields. Soon the family will gather around the table to celebrate Thanksgiving. From near and far, over the river and through the woods to my house they will come.

Let's do a head count of who won't be coming this year, though. Aunt Phoebe is in a nursing home. Grandma Bess has passed—God rest her soul. Karen won't come if Sue is here, and Sue won't come if Karen is here. Cousin Lin is stuck in the snow. Flo's cat is too sick for Flo to go anywhere. Airline tickets are just too high for nephew Sky and his six kids. Leave the extra table leaf and the chairs downstairs.

Time to take out the finery kept in a special place for just this occasion. Grandma's gold-rimmed English precious china, Mom's linen embroidered table cloths, my sterling wedding silverware, and the fine cut Waterford crystal goblets handed down through three generations.

Except the china can't go in the microwave; the linens need ironing; and the crystal must be hand-washed. Change in plans: the paper plates from Walmart with the cute little turkeys on them will go well with the plastic tablecloth, knives, spoons, and forks.

Bring out those time-tested recipes handed down from mother to daughter, to daughter, to daughter. The memory of the aroma of the many predictable foods make my taste buds start to salivate. Turkey basting in its buttery juice, topped by a rich gravy; fresh cranberry sauce with its tangy flavor; creamy mashed potatoes suffocating in milk and butter; spicy flavored sweet potatoes topped with nuts and marshmallows; stacks of fresh warm rolls; and those wonderful desserts—sugary and spicy pumpkin and apple pies topped with towers of homemade whipped cream.

However, Kay, Allie, and Jordan are vegetarians, Gordon is allergic to nuts, Melissa only eats organic, Ted is lactose intolerant, Julie eats gluten free,

Peggy eats no spice, Phil eats no meat, Liz eats no sweets, the baby throws everything on the floor, and the dog is too old to eat.

Oh hell, I think I'll just make a reservation down the street.

# The Treasure

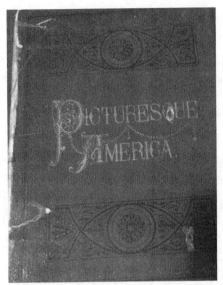

She really shouldn't be so critical of the man she took after, but once again he blew it. Big time now. It was a flaw in their personalities that caused the problem. She and her dad were more concerned with finishing a job then getting it done perfectly. Though her sister and her mother spent forever working on a project, never ever satisfied with it, and thus hardly ever finishing one, that would have been better in this case.

Contemplating what she should do next, she rose and walked over to the kitchen counter, and stared at the rain beating against the window.

With a newly made chocolate chip cookie in one hand and a cup of hot coffee in the other, she sat back down at the table, staring from the book sitting in front of her to the eBay computer page. Squinting, she tried to enlarge the page to make sure she had read it correctly. Since her cataract surgery her sight had never been the same. Her dad had complained about the same thing, though he was old by then. Or had he been around 70—her own age, now? Oh well.

Running her finger over the worn leather cover of the book, she thought about the first time she had an inkling that her father wasn't the best fixer-upper in the whole wide world. She always thought the man who had glued her doll back together after she had fallen and dropped it was wonderful—but her mom didn't always agree with her.

Her father could do wonders with glue, even before the new super glues were invented. Of course if he hadn't dropped mom's big cut glass bowl—the one her grandmother had left them, the one that always sat at the center of the dining room table, the one mom kept sparkling clean—he wouldn't have had to glue it back together.

Actually, when she thought about it, her mom had been angrier when dad tried to move the white chalk statue of the peasant boy that sat atop the black marble pedestal. It was even harder to glue that one back together after it rolled down two flights of stairs. Luckily, mom yelled for her to get out of the way, or her fingers and toes might have been chopped off like those of the poor peasant boy.

She never glued anything back together. If she broke it, she sent it out to be fixed, or she just threw it away, something she should do with mom's chipped Limoges cup that she held in her hand. Mom had told her not to put fine china in the dishwasher, but she was always in a hurry, and forgot. Oh well.

Maybe her dad should have stuck with his woodworking hobby. Her dad made the most beautiful wooden book shelves for her playroom. Then again, maybe he should have hired someone like mom always begged him to do. She had been thrilled with her book shelves even though dad used the new red-metal trimmed kitchen table as a base to saw the wood on. It never bothered her that a piece of the table forever after was missing, but it did upset her mom.

Into the front room she roamed, where she glanced at the picture of her dad that sat on the mantel with the other family pictures. He was a handsome man—tall, slim, with a salt-and-pepper mustache circling his smiling face. She did miss his loud, boisterous voice echoing through the phone on his daily calls, his crushing hug, and the words "I love you" that ended every call and visit.

Her mind wandered back to the book. When she saw it on eBay she had gotten very excited. It wasn't only the money; it was the thrill of finding a treasure. Quickly she had run up the steps and rolled down the box of old books from her storage closet. The faint smell of mildew made her slow down. Dad had been gone more than fifteen years, and this box had been stored in his basement for several years prior, before it found a home at her abode. Maybe her memory was wrong; maybe the astonishing pictures he had shown her so many years ago actually belonged to another book, long gone.

Sitting cross-legged on the floor she slowly rummaged through the big cardboard box, tossing books and papers out until she finally found it.

Yes, right there in her hand was the book *Picturesque America* from 1872. The same book that sold on eBay for $12,000. Well, almost the same one. Since the one she was holding in her hand had belonged to her dad, that meant it wasn't in perfect shape.

First of all, she had only one of the two volumes—and the one she held had been both taped and glued back together, upside down.

That was dad. She smiled, shook her head, and stared at her dad's picture. It took her a few minutes before she realized her real treasure was the collection of memories of a dad who may not have been perfect, but one who knew how to pass on his love. Memories she could pass on to her children and grandchildren.

And those were and always would be in perfect condition.

# The Unknown

The unknown was making her heart beat too fast, her head pound, and her ability to concentrate void.

She clenches her teeth and paces back and forth. In front of her sit two phones—the home line and her cell phone. They promised to call this morning. It is one o'clock in the afternoon. And so far, nothing.

The sharp, loud whistle of the tea kettle distracts her. Maybe another cup of tea will help. She pours the steaming water from the kettle into one of her delicate flowered Limoges cups. Use them, she thinks. The children will just toss all her treasures to the wind. This generation moves so much: they want no baggage—just give them the cash!

She dips the teabag three times, and adds a little milk and sugar. Just the way her grandmother taught her to do.

A second before the cup reaches her lips, one of the phones rings. She grabs it with trembling hands.

"Will you accept a collect call from the county jail?" an operator asks.

"Are you crazy?" she screams. The cup drops from her hands. On the floor lay a million pieces of dainty china. She sits down, drops her head in her hands, and cries—for grandma's cup, and for her fears.

She holds the cell phone in her right hand and talks to it. "Ring already," she says. "I can't stand this not knowing. Tell me, and I can deal with it. Do I have breast cancer?" She inadvertently feels her left breast with her left hand.

She starts to pace again. She knows it's cancer. She has no illusions. The verdict has been in for years. How can it not be cancer? Her grandmother, her aunt, and her mother died of breast cancer. It is her destiny. Most likely women in Russia from the Weinberg family died from breast cancer for centuries, way before they had a name to describe the disease. She was old by her family's standard—at 66. The other women in her family all were gone by their 56th birthday.

She carefully sweeps up the broken china, and tosses the shards into the garbage. She notices a tiny piece on the counter, and grabs for it. She jumps at the sharp sting, and soon notices the bright red blood trickling down her hand. She heads to the bathroom for a bandage.

She is reminded of the endless blood tests her mother had to endure. She can hear her mother's whisper of a voice begging the nurse to use a butterfly needle because her veins were small. Towards the end there were no veins left to draw blood from. Her mother was bruised with black, blue, and red marks on each arm, each hand, each foot.

Yes, today they have the port, but back in the early 1970s it was stick after stick after stick. Her mother was so young, only 52.

Memory moves back and forth between a mother in agony and pain, and a young girl of 26, newly married, living in a world between disease and death, and diapers and a new life. She didn't understand; in fact, she was angry back then. Just when she needed a mother to help her with her newborn she was thrust into the role of caretaker. She was too young for the double job.

A phone rings again. She rushes towards the kitchen. This time she checks the caller ID. It is her friend, Barbra. She lets it ring. Today she has no time for idle conversation. She has told no one, not even her son in California. No need to talk about it until the verdict is in.

She moves to the window. Virgin snow covers the ground, and there is a cardinal at the feeder. The bird's crimson red against the snow as the orange sun sneaks through the horizon makes a beautiful picture.

She thinks about how her mother always made sure the birds were fed, even when she cried from pain, nausea, clumps of soft black curly hairs lying on her pillow, no energy, and most of all from the loss of her entire left breast. Yes, back in the early '70s torture, the act of making someone die a slow death in agony went by another name—chemotherapy.

My grandmother was much luckier, she tells herself. One day her breast was double its size, and four months later she was gone. Twenty years later, mother lasted two years. They tell me the surgery and treatment are much easier now. They can keep you alive much longer, with less torture, and even cure some of us. Well, we'll see.

She goes to the refrigerator, takes out a bagel, and drops it in the toaster. She has hardly slept or eaten since the mammogram led to the biopsy. Her hands are shaking as she butters the bagel.

She can't stand it any longer. She picks up the phone and calls the doctor's office. The nurse answers, and says, "Dr. Wall was about to call you. I'll get him."

It feels like an eternity until the doctor comes on the line. "Shelly, we have good news about your breast. The biopsy was clear. You do not have breast cancer, but we would like you to come into the hospital for an angiogram. The ultrasound looks like there is blockage to your heart."

She holds the phone close to her ear. "Are you sure I don't have breast cancer?"

The doctor answers, "You do not have breast cancer, but you could have a heart attack if you're not treated."

"You're wrong, doctor; no woman in my family had heart trouble. We have breast cancer in my family."

She hangs up and smiles. Her uncle, the doctor, used to ask why can't this family die of a nice clean heart attack, instead of being tortured by cancer? Maybe she'll be the one to break the cancer curse!

# Animal Magnetism

# Cat-ching On

I've been trying hard to make Tyrone into a dog, but it just isn't working.

Having been a dog person for the majority of my 60-some odd years, I really don't know what to do with a cat.

Why do I have Tyrone? An empty nester, retired and living in the country, I wanted no more pets to take care of and worry about. Then this adorable black and white tabby started to hang around, and I fed him.

You know how that goes. After spending money on shots and surgery to get him neutered, I had to let him move in.

I reasoned that it was a good idea to have an animal around to help protect me. With fond memories I thought about how our collie, Charley, barked loudly and circled around any visitors before letting them near me.

Tyrone is almost as big as a small coyote, and as fierce as any predator. I watched him narrow his eyes, hiss fiercely, and stretch out his paws when the neighbor's cat dared to step on our property.

So I felt safe having him around—that is until a stranger rang our doorbell and Tyrone made a beeline for unknown parts. When I called him he looked back with an expression that said, "Lady, you are on your own. I take care of myself only!"

The most disturbing part of having a cat, as opposed to a dog, is the cat's ability to jump. Here I was entertaining some new neighbors with a gourmet lunch, when I noticed the cat extending his body and surveying the table top. Being new to cats, I hadn't realized he was planning to jump up onto the middle of the table, upsetting my food and dishes.

Just think, all those years I thought it was so terrible when my dog jumped up and greeted my guests at the door. A few hairs of fur on a guest were nothing compared to a splattered plate of pasta.

After the guests left, Tyrone wouldn't even eat the ruined food. He ate only fancy cat food or tuna. Charlie would have cleaned up the food off the floor and finished the leftovers.

Tyrone had lived the first half of his life outdoors, so it was virtually impossible to keep him inside or to trim down his claws. Dogs were kept in place by leashes, and fences, and I never had to worry about my dogs getting lost. Now I was spending days calling Tyrone, and looking around our three acres for him.

Of course he never responded to my calls. A dog comes when you call him, and a cat comes when he is ready.

On the plus side, cats do not need to be walked. They adjust to litter boxes easily, and they can be left alone for days. They make very little noise, and they don't need the same level of attention dogs need. In fact, sometimes I think Tyrone does me a favor by letting me play with him and pet him.

When he is done he just curls up and goes to sleep. If I should wake him to start playing again, he will hiss and reach out with a sharp claw poised to strike.

Come to think of it, he reminds me of my husband.

# Charlie, Our Therapist

"I'm very sorry, there is nothing else we can do. His heart is giving out."

"I want to take him home," I answered. As the veterinarian carefully put Charlie, my beautiful collie, in the car, my mind raced back twelve years.

My twelve-year-old son, Jeff, had just died of leukemia, and I was in a deep depression. A few months before he died, my husband had brought home a collie puppy. I resented the full-of-life puppy and paid little attention to him until I found myself home alone with him.

My husband, Sam, was back to work, and my younger son, Mike, was back in school. No one could get me out of bed. That is, no one but this six-month-old puppy. He proceeded to bark and jump all over me. When I became angry, he would lay down near me, wag his tail, and lick my cheek. I finally was forced to get out of bed to feed and walk him.

After several weeks, in spite of my complaining, I began to warm up to Charlie. He had a fluffy mahogany-and-white coat. His paws were huge for a puppy. They gave a hint of the large, dignified, and stately adult collie he would become. When I walked him, everyone in the neighborhood stopped to pet my friendly, vivacious puppy. The bank gave him doggy cookies, and the ice cream parlor gave him vanilla cones.

Charlie was full of the same mischief as our other puppies had been. He tore socks, slept on the sofa, and swallowed anything on the ground or floor, including a battery. The battery-swallowing incident became the first of many trips to the veterinarian. We believe, though it was never proven, that Charlie also was instrumental in the toilet drowning of our beloved parakeet, Chicken.

We did notice that Charlie was a quick study. He learned to alert us when he needed to go out. He understood when he was reprimanded, and did not repeat an offense. Mike taught him many tricks, such as rolling over and playing dead, retrieving balls and sticks, and even how to climb up on the ladder to the top bunk bed. Unfortunately he never learned how to get down by himself. He loved to sleep in a bed with his head on the pillow.

Therapy was recommended for the family after Jeff died. We didn't need it, because we had our own in-house therapist: Charlie. We could talk and talk and pour our hearts out to him for hours. He listened attentively and gave unconditional love. He settled down to being a gentle, kind, and intuitive friend.

Charlie had a soul. He was my husband's cross-country ski partner, my son's lost brother, my father's grandchild, and my constant companion. He joined us on shopping trips and vacations. He loved running loose in the neighboring forest preserves. A photographer we came across in the woods once asked to take his picture. Charlie became a star when his photo appeared on the cover of the neighborhood telephone book.

At age eleven, he became very tired and sluggish. After a run with Sam in the forest preserve, he collapsed. A trip to the veterinarian showed a heart problem. Charlie was put on a diet and on heart medicine. He was not happy.

I must admit that I let him cheat some. He really missed people-food, especially his ice cream cones. After a year of medicine, things went downhill.

We made an appointment to see a heart specialist at the University of Illinois veterinary clinic in Urbana, Illinois. This was a hundred miles south of our home. A cardiogram, blood test, and a CAT scan only produced a large doctor's bill. The tests confirmed our neighborhood veterinarian's diagnosis of terminal heart failure. I asked if surgery was an option. I was willing to spend anything on this grown puppy that I once resented. But it was not an option. We headed for home.

"Charlie, get out of the car. You can make it," I heard my dad yell as I was walking into the house to get Sam. My dad and I had just come back from that last trip to the veterinarian. As Sam walked out ready to carry Charlie into the house, we saw my 85-year-old heart patient dad and my twelve-year-old heart patient collie slowly walk into the house together.

Charlie died five hours later, surrounded by his therapy patients. It was time to join Jeff and for Charlie to report to him that Mike was safely away at college, and Mom, Dad, and Grandpa were finally doing much better.

I don't know if it's true that all dogs go to Heaven, but I definitely know it's true for Charlie.

# Into the Woods

The bushy-tailed red fox with her ears twitching stared at me through glowing brown eyes. I waited—still as could be except for the beating of my heart—until as suddenly as she appeared, she was gone, back into the thick, dark, shadowy woods.

Was she looking for prey? Had she been the one who had killed the poor soft cuddly baby rabbits? Did she have a nest nearby with babies who needed food too? Had I chewed out my cat for something he hadn't done?

Life in my woods was chaotic for the creatures living here, from the insects swirling around in the night sky to the white opossum blindly searching for food, to me, the human frantically searching for my 16-year-old tabby cat.

Walking around in the woods at night was not one of my favorite things to do, but my beloved pet had run away and I would do most anything to find him.

I had no idea how long I had trudged through the woods adjacent to my property, calling his name. Only thinking of finding my cat, I had left the sweater—the one that could be warming my rapidly chilling bones—on the chair in my kitchen. Instead, I had grabbed a can of tuna, hoping to lure my cat with the fishy odor and succulent taste he loves so much.

Taking my cell phone and a flashlight would have been smart, too, but hindsight is 20/20. I hadn't realized how soon that beautiful orange glow of the sun could disappear and deep dark night would take over, especially on an evening when the moon was throwing off just a mere sliver of light.

The terrifying howl of coyotes sent chills down my spine. I hoped it was the cool clear night that made the barks and howls echo from a more distant place than the woods in which I was walking. The shriek that came from my trembling lips was meant to scare off a possible attacking coyote, not for the tall, erect, glowing-eyed doe who whisked by me.

I had had enough. My beloved woods took on a different feel at night. I would have to continue my search tomorrow, I thought, as I beelined as fast as I could back to my home. Panting for breath, I slowed my run down to nearly a crawl as I approached my front porch.

To my surprise, a tabby cat stood up from his prone position on the concrete stoop and proceeded to give me an indignant meow. I think he said, "Where were you?"

Cats know the value of staying close to home, even if we humans forget it sometimes.

# Ode to Tyrone

Tyrone, you are the greatest contortionist I've ever met.

I can watch you change positions in your feline sleep for hours. Your slim, trim, muscular body stretched across the bouncy pink sofa pulls in like a tight ball one minute, only to slowly unfold legs across your soft tummy the next. This produces the most unusual positions.

Just a quiet "swoosh" of a whisper from my lips will make your ears perk up at attention, resulting in your incredible hearing waking up all your senses.

Those large, bright, glowing green eyes can easily mesmerize anyone who dares to stare into them. The slightest movement across your field of vision will cause a speedy swat from your sharp, needle-like claws.

You are a cunning hunter, almost always capturing your prey—sometimes for food, but mostly for play now that you've been spoiled by fancy cat food and tuna.

Heaven help any other cat who invades your territory. I watch you speed out the back door in the early morning, sniffing around to make sure only the resident squirrels, birds, raccoons, and deer have been around

So much of your day is spent using your specialized tongue to keep your soft, lustrous coat clean and shiny.

There is a gentle, loving part to you also. A gentle rubbing of your head and ears will calm you down and produce a low, constant purring sound. Then you will become my loving companion.

But true to your cat nature, it will always be you, not I, who will decide when it is time to move on.

# Tyrone Is No More

My eyes disbelieved when I looked at the time
The clock on the dresser registered half past nine
Someone has told it Tyrone is no more.

No claws scratching, no high-pitch meowing
The house is silent this dreary morning
Someone has told it Tyrone is no more.

Pecking at seeds I've dropped on the patio floor
The little birds are swaggering up to my door
Someone has told them Tyrone is no more.

The squirrels are swinging here and there without a care
The orange cat is frolicking in the snow, no reason for him to go
Someone has told them Tyrone is no more.

No water bowl to change, no litter box to clean
My kitchen today is very pristine
Someone has told it Tyrone is no more.

I sat on the sofa with no fear
That my clothing would be covered with fur from there to here
Someone has told it Tyrone is no more.

I opened the door as wide as can be, for today no cat will sneak out on me
So the chipmunks and mice were dancing with glee
Someone has told them Tyrone is no more.

I reached out my hand to caress my cat
It stayed there outreached with no one to pat
My eyes filled with tears, and my heart tore
Because Tyrone is no more.

# There Is a Frog in my Pool

There is a frog in my pool
Believe me it's true
He is very green without an ounce of blue
He swims all around
The water is so clear he can easily be found
He hops and jumps in and out
The water splashes all about
The air is so nice now that he is here
Not a fly, not a bug, not a mosquito is left for me to fear
There is a frog in my pool.

# Why I Can't Get Another Pet

Sam and I have been married for 48 years. During 44 of those years we've been pet owners. We've had collie dogs, tabby cats, parrots, some exotic fish, and way too many hamsters. In fact some hamsters may still be hiding in our former home. Not my problem anymore!

Our pets have been our loving companions.

Prince was the collie that helped us raise our young boys, and Charlie was our family's therapist after Jeff died. JoJo was the parrot that kept everyone out of the house and Chicken the sweetest bird of all.

Mama and Tyrone were the cats that taught us how to deal with an empty nest and life in the country.

I must admit it is hard being petless. The house feels very quiet and still without the pitter-patter of paws, or the loving greeting at the door of a dog who misses us, or of a cat who acts as if he doesn't care. There are the chipmunks scurrying by me while I am on the patio, and the two frogs swimming with me in the pool, the squirrels and birds competing for the seeds in the feeders, but no one to sit by me indoors and rub against my legs.

The ADT alarm system has never been as reassuring as the bark or the hissing of one of our furry friends when a stranger was nearby.

Unconditional love is what a pet gives. Doesn't matter what you look like, how much money or power you possess—that pet loves you for you. Though food does help keep that unconditional love intact.

Attachment, love, then heartache when that pet becomes ill and dies. We've been there too many times to start all over again.

Our granddaughter has been trying to get us to adopt and to give a loving home to another dog or cat. She is one of those people who loves animals, and is constantly fostering, and finding homes for the homeless creatures.

I know she means well, but we're not ready to take that step. I've given her my stock excuses: We are too old, we travel too much. But I haven't told her my real reason, which is: We've gained too much weight to share our bed with a pet!

I'll never know how we managed to get a night's sleep with a 90-lb. Collie, or to be intimate with each other while one cat was laying across Sam's middle, and the other one was purring in my ear.

We are at an age where we need to spread out and sleep at least eight hours a night. Dogs and cats are night prowlers, too. Sometimes they bark, sometimes they purr, sometimes they even snore, and most of all they are territorial. Once they have claimed our bed we're in big trouble. It would be the floor for us.

And at 72 or more, once we've hit the floor we'll never get up!

# Feeding a Stray Kitten
# That I Really Don't Need

*I don't want another cat. I really don't!*

Why did I move out to the country where the farmers let their cats multiply and stray? I need to move back to the city where the cats are afraid to be on the streets.

*I don't want another cat. I really don't!*

She looks so pathetic out there in the rain. She must be around six months old. What is wrong with you? A kitten when you are in your seventies? She could outlive you. Although, I could leave her money in my will, then she will be taken care of when I die.

*I don't want another cat. I really don't!*

The poor thing devoured the food. She must be starving. How could people be so cruel to their pets?

*I don't want another cat. I really don't!*

We travel too much. My kids are in Arizona. She is a pretty thing—a calico cat. I've only had tabbies. She let me pet her before running away.

*I don't want another cat. I really don't!*

She will have to be vaccinated and neutered, and I will have to find someone to watch her when we are gone. Oh, the expense and the worry!

What about the furniture? I bet she is a scratcher.

*I don't want another cat. I really don't!*

I could take her to a no-kill shelter. She is so young and cute I'm sure she will be adopted. Though many shelters are not accepting cats because there are so many. Can one really trust a no-kill?

*I don't want another cat. I really don't!*

Fur all over the house, dirt on the floor, allergic friends, rips on everything, no room in your own bed, and no more sleeping to 9 a.m.

*I don't want another cat. I really don't!*

No chipmunk problem outside, just a cat problem inside. No mouse problem either. Look at those bright black eyes begging to come in where it is warm.

*I don't want another cat. I really don't! But what can I do?*

# The Passing Parade

# The Congress to Make Humans

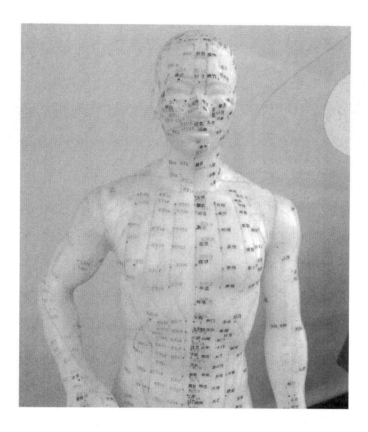

God to the Angels: We've been fighting over how to make these humans for six days and six nights. I want to rest tomorrow, so let's finish the negotiations.

Angels: Let's start with toes and fingers.

God: Fifteen toes and fifteen fingers. Are you crazy?

Angels: What's wrong with that?

God: The number is uneven. They will never figure it out.

Angels: Then let's make them smart enough to figure it out.

God: A few can be smarter, but we have to keep the majority dumb.

Angels: Why?

God: Somebody has to do the dirty cleanup jobs.

Angels: Why?

God: We don't want a dirty planet. It wouldn't look good when mom comes to visit.

Angels: Okay, we'll go with your ten fingers and ten toes, if you will let us put 206 bones in them.

God: Two hundred and six bones, are you crazy?

Angels: Listen, they will need spares. The bags of bones you bought are seconds, and they will break easily.

God: You have them with two of most organs, but only one heart. Why?

Angels: It got too complicated to route all that blood in two directions, so we gave up.

God: I think all humans should be pink.

Angels: No, blue would be better.

God: We already used all the dye on the plants and animals. We only have so much money to spend.

Angels: Ok, so what color should we use?

God: How about brown? We have a lot of brown left over. What about different shades of brown from almost white to almost black?

Angels: I really miss giving them some color. What about making the toes different colors?

God: What's with you and toes?

Angels: Listen, we have a little blue and green left over. Not enough for toes, but maybe enough for the eyes.

God: Now the tough part. I don't want to be bothered constantly making new humans when the old ones wear out.

Angels: So let's give them organs to reproduce on their own.

God: Where should we put the organs?

Angels: Put them anywhere. They will only use them a few times when they want to have children!

# Hilltop Winter

Here I am sitting in the house the whole damn cold, snowy, dreary winter with a sick cat who can't eat, while I can't stop eating. As I finish another brownie I start telling myself to stop, but somehow my hands and mouth refuse to listen to my brain.

If I stay away from the scale I will have no idea if I've gained any weight. Who can tell when you spend the day in sweats or a bathrobe anyway? In the old days before retirement I had to dress decently and make it out the door. Not anymore.

Anyway, it is just not worth trying to battle the ice and snow on the hill where I live. Or on our cars. We haven't put a car in the garage in 30 years—it is loaded with bicycles, tires, tools, and other stuff we never use, while our four old cars sit outside covered with snow, all with batteries that die in cold weather.

Eighteen years ago I thought that buying a house on a hill was charming, but now at 71, that hill leaves me in fear of broken bones. Old brittle bones creak and crack easily. Break a major one and you are done for. Just a broken toe has caused me to put all my beautiful expensive high heels on the shelf where I can admire them from a distance only.

Being stuck inside for four months can make one stir crazy. Cabinets and drawers have been cleaned, books have been read, games played on the Internet, and all conversation between me and my husband put at a standstill.

Thank God—otherwise, we might kill each other because of too much togetherness!

We even tried sex but hell, we're in our seventies, and we were worried if we got too frisky that the ambulance would have trouble getting up the icy hill. So here I am cooking, baking, and eating again.

Actually, the beloved spring to which I've so looked forward is on my dread list, because I will have to fit into real clothes and eventually a bathing suit.

I'd better get a Krispy Kreme doughnut before I go into a deep depression!

# Lights, Camera, Catharsis

I am sitting on a soft maroon leather sofa across from a large wooden desk. Hard, bright lights are blaring on me, making me very warm. The studio is much smaller than I thought it would be. Efficient people are moving around with cameras and papers. A tall, thin man wearing a very expensive salt-and-pepper hairpiece, a navy blue suit, and a red tie, enters the room. He walks toward me and shakes my hand.

"Five minutes and we are on. Are you okay?" he asks, as he takes his place by the desk.

I shake my head and answer, "Yes."

I'd better be okay. I've spent close to a week preparing for this day. My blue dress with a simple strand of pearls was selected after trying on half of my closet. My straight gray hair was professionally cut and styled in a pageboy. It lays just right. Instead of my usual five-minute makeup job, I sat patiently while an artist spent 50 minutes transforming my 70-year-old face into that of a 50-year-old model; eyes bright and shiny, skin wrinkle-free and smooth with just a touch of a warm glow, and dark pink lipstick drawn on without a smudge.

This was my first television appearance with a famous interviewer. After 20 years of writing, my latest novel has made me an overnight success!

I spent two days re-reading my novel, taking notes as if I were a school child taking a course. I needed to make sure I remembered the names, connections, and dates. I was once embarrassed by a radio interviewer who questioned my description of a 1950s car. Besides the details in the book I was prepared to answer the normal questions such as, "Tell me about your new book," or, "How did you get started writing?"

Perry Carleton did his opening shtick, and then welcomed me. He turned away from the cameras, and stared into my face with his large brown eyes.

"Susan, your first five books are murder mysteries, following a familiar pattern, though some have some very gruesome characters," he said. "Your new book is very different. Why?"

"Perry, I felt like it was time to branch out," I answered. "My novel, *Friends*, was written for the women who have depended on each through the years."

Perry brought his cup of coffee to his lips and took a sip before saying, "Susan, I believe this book is your biography."

He sent an emotional wave through my body. My voice cracked as I answered. "The book is fiction, and in fiction one can let her mind run wild. Of course there is some of an author's personality and history in everything she writes."

His face took on a devilish grin. "There are four women in the story. I would like to know which woman you are.

"Are you Alice, the very spiritual, loyal, and understanding friend?

"Are you Cate, the headstrong, sexy kitten always showing her cleavage and creating trouble?

"Are you Carol, the very efficient, proper, and frustrated lady?

"Or are you Dina, the quiet, strong, and very loyal lady?"

I swallowed hard and lowered my face, staring at the floor. I hadn't expected someone who had actually read my book in depth. I expected Perry to be an arrogant celebrity who wouldn't have given up his time. I thought he would refer to notes an aide had made for him, but there were no notes on his desk.

I was feeling warm, and very nervous. "Perry, I told you the book is fiction," I answered a little too harshly.

"Come on Susan," he shot back. "You haven't answered my question." He turned to the audience and said, "Audience, clap if you want to know which woman is modeled after Susan?"

As the audience clapped I slid down in my seat.

Perry turned from the audience to me with his arms opened, questioning.

I took a deep breath, and said, "None of the above. I was the little girl."

"The little girl?" he answered quizzically.

"Yes, the perfect little girl, Carol's daughter," I revealed. "The little girl who could do nothing wrong because her proper mother would be disappointed in her."

"That little girl drowned herself in the novel," Perry remembered. "Did you ever think of suicide?"

"Never," I answered, restraining myself from adding the words, "until now." What I said was, "Instead I became a writer who could let her characters be sex fiends, murderers, rebels, terrible or wonderful people, and I could live through them."

And then I recited a poem:

### Your Voice Echoes in My Head
*"Be kind, be nice, and above all else continue to please*
*Then new friends you will develop with ease"*
*Your voice still echoes through my head*
*Something I'm afraid will continue until I'm dead*

*From the depths of my soul*
*I wish I could let go*
*A scream, a yell, a stomp of my shoe*
*If only I could tell someone to go to hell, too*

*My pain, anger, and loss of hope continue to stay inside*
*Headaches, stomachaches, lack of strength and pride*
*Only tell that my head still is in the sand, you see*
*How I wish I could just be me*

*But your voice still echoes in my head*
*Something I'm afraid will continue until I'm dead.*

A deeply personal revelation punctuated by a poem made for some great TV that evening. Perry sat back with a look that was both flabbergasted and pleased.

I think I had the same look—flabbergasted that I had revealed 70 years of pain on TV, and pleased that I had finally gotten it off my chest.

# The Metra Train

I wandered into this particular Metra commuter train car by accident. Seldom had I ridden in the first car behind the engine, but today the temperature in Chicago was in the low teens and I wanted to get off the train as close as possible to where my car was parked.

I was on my way home from downtown on one of the late rush hour trains. My trip was going to take one hour and forty minutes. Now that I'd relocated to the country, I had to travel from the first stop to the last—Union Station in Chicago to Fox Lake, a town near the Wisconsin border.

I joked to friends that now I could nap and not miss my stop, or finally finish the book *War and Peace*. I was thankful that my editing job required me to take the train only three days a week. The rest of the time I could work from home.

My step into the first car on the 5:33 would change my life. I sat down on the worn red vinyl seats towards the middle of the car, away from most of the other passengers who seemed to be lumped together in the front seats.

My phone battery was almost dead, and I had finished my book in the morning on the way downtown, so I found myself eavesdropping on the group of a half-dozen other occupants. They were a noisy bunch, laughing and joking. Probably a group of friends who were traveling home from some event in the city, I thought. This was a typical good-weather group, like you see when the Chicago Cubs are playing. Of course, there were no baseball games this time of year.

On taking a closer look, I noticed they really didn't seem like a homogenous group. The people were young, old, well-dressed, and shabbily outfitted—all adults.

"Didn't I get your ticket in the quiet car?" asked a voice that made me jump. It was the conductor.

"Yes," I almost shouted. All eyes looked our way.

I slid back into my seat as the conductor moved to the front of the car, where he was warmly greeted by the others.

The conductor, around six feet tall and well padded around the middle, sat down facing the group. "Okay, today's joke," he said. "Why did the chicken cross the road?"

A disheveled, brown-haired, bearded guy looked up with a sneer, and said, "Are you kidding? I've been waiting all day for one of your real jokes." He took a drink from the can of beer he was holding.

The conductor looked towards the middle of the car, where I was sitting. All eyes turned my way.

I raised my hands in a surrendering gesture, and said, "Don't let me interfere with anything."

A stocky, bald-headed man, probably in his fifties, walked back to where I was sitting. He held out a bag of pretzels, offering me some. "In the good old days, there used to be a snack car where we would hang out," he explained. "Now we have to bring our own, and reserve one of the less occupied cars."

I took a pretzel from his bag, noticing the calluses on hands that indicated he was a manual laborer. "Thanks," I said.

"I haven't seen you before," he replied. "Are you new on this line?"

"I just moved from the city to Lake Geneva, near Fox Lake," I explained. "I'll be on this train three days a week. I could move back a car."

"Make Friday one of those days," he said. "Once a month is pizza Friday."

He didn't invite me up front, or request that I move, so I stayed where I was, pretending to read, catching a conversation or a joke here or there.

I scrutinized the group from afar, especially the two women. One was a blonde with shoulder-length hair and too much make-up. The other was older, with dark eyebrows, black hair, and narrow glasses over a slender nose. It was impossible to check their figures, or their clothing, which was covered by winter coats.

Individuals from the group started to depart the train one or two stops before the end of the line, each time saying to each other, "See you tomorrow," indicating they were commuters who had become train friends. Only two of the group left with me at the end of the line. Both men gave me a friendly nod.

I was a newly divorced empty-nester who had decided to move from the high-living city to the Lake Geneva vacation condo I had won in our divorce settlement. The farthest away I could get from my wandering husband and his girlfriend was my goal—one I questioned when I started to make the long commute to work.

Today was the first day I had left the train with a smile. By the time I walked to parking space number 85, shoveled the snow off my car, warmed the heater, and drove the twenty miles to Lake Geneva, it would be close to eight o'clock. But instead of my usual cursing of the commute, I was looking forward to Friday and pizza day—whatever that meant.

Friday, I left my office in a hurry; I didn't want to miss my 5:33 train. The snow was still on the ground, but the temperature was in the thirties as I raced down Adams Street to Union Station. As it turned out, I was the second one in car number one.

My bald-headed friend waved his arm for me to come to the front of the car. I sat down next to him and asked, "Tell me a little about the group."

"I'm Larry, originally from the Polish neighborhood in South Chicago," he recounted. "When the steel mills started to close, my cousin Kenny got me a job hauling junk and moved me up to Round Lake with his family. He's the skinny guy who sits with me.

"Brad, the good-looking, classy dresser who just walked in the car is a big-shot lawyer. He wandered into the car like you did. I never know what he is talking about half the time. The dark-haired broad works with him. She is an icicle, thinks she's too good for us.

"Here comes Sasha—she's Polish like me. A good-looker, and funny. She laughs at everything. Works as a housekeeper in one of the buildings. We go out for a beer together every once and a while," Larry concluded.

Soon all seven commuters were seated, and the train was on its way.

Larry turned to the group, and said "This is…" He stopped and looked at me, saying, "Hey, what's your name?"

"Jessica," I answered.

The travelers nodded and started talking to each other about work, the news, and life in general. I wasn't sure if I was accepted until they stopped and listened to my opinion on a current event.

Sasha, who still had an accent, told me, "Jessica! We stopped to listen to you this time, but if you want to be heard you better speak up louder, and jump right in to the conversation."

Larry held up his hand. "I need money," he announced. "We just passed Deerfield. Four dollars, everyone." I knitted my eyebrows as I asked, "For what?"

"For the pizza," he answered as the train stopped at the Lake Forest Station, where a delivery man handed Larry a Lou Malnati's pizza in exchange for twenty-four dollars. Then seven occupants, plus the conductor, who magically appeared at that moment, sat down to a mouth-watering deep-dish pizza dinner. The last Friday of the month was indeed Pizza Friday, and I tried to be there from then on.

The group taught me the ins and outs of commuter travel. You have to come early to get a good parking spot; always bring water and toilet paper, as the toilets never have either; carry a flashlight and comfortable shoes (they once had to hoof it from a broken-down train in between stations, they explained); have a charged phone for an emergency, or for when the train is late, which happens often; get to know the conductor, he can be helpful.

Charley, a friend of Larry's, joined the group a few weeks later. Sasha, who was growing bigger by the day, finally announced she was pregnant. No husband was ever mentioned, and Larry staunchly denied that the baby could be his.

Sasha continued to work through her ninth month when, on the day we planned to give her a baby shower, she delivered the baby right on the train—with the help of her friends, including new friend Charley, who turned out to be a hospital orderly with five kids of his own. After a few months away, Sasha met us with the baby at the Round Lake Station so we could see him.

Judy, the dark-haired icicle who hardly talked, suddenly stopped joining us. Brad said one day she announced that she was quitting her law office, and no one knew why. She didn't answer her phone or e-mails, so we forgot about her until Brad, teary-eyed and upset, passed around the obituary section of the *Chicago Tribune.* Judy, who we all misjudged as being cold and arrogant, had been battling ovarian cancer for two years. I went with Brad to Judy's funeral

One deceptively bright and sunny spring day, while the train was pulling into the Lake Cook station, the inhabitants of the first car witnessed a horrible tragedy. A young lady busy talking on her cell phone ran in front of the train.

There wasn't much left of her. Disconnected limbs, eyes, hair, clothing, blood, and broken teeth were scattered across the tracks. The sirens from the police cars and ambulances echoed in our ears, and the train was immobile for forty-five minutes. We tried not to look out the windows, but we, and the crowd that had gathered by the station, found ourselves mesmerized. No one cried, and no one spoke. Our minds tried to file the image as fiction, like a movie, or a computer game—not reality.

I don't know about my other commuter friends but, haunted by that memory, I never went back on the Fox Lake train. I worked at home or occasionally I drove downtown. Maybe I would have gone back to the train eventually, but I accepted a new job in Arizona near my son and family.

I really wanted to contact my fellow commuters, but in the three years I had traveled three times per week with them in car number one, I learned only their first names and commuter stops. Even with the Internet, that wasn't enough information to find them.

I guess some people are only meant to be situational friends.

# People Watching

I watched her the whole time she worked with her small compact mirror.

Why not? I had nothing else to do. The train ride from Union Station in downtown Chicago to Fox Lake lasted one hour and forty minutes. I had planned to read on my iPad but alas, it was sitting in my car in the parking lot. Raindrops pounded against the dark, dirty windows, so landscape viewing was not an option. But people watching always is.

Before I spotted the woman with the mirror, my gaze had zoomed in on a tall, thin fellow wearing a heavy winter jacket. He seemed to be mumbling to himself. It was the middle of the summer, so the jacket aroused my suspicions, but the mumbling could just be a man talking on a hidden digital device. So I couldn't label him crazy—yet. Or ever, since my observations were interrupted when he exited at the next station. I had to look for someone else to analyze.

My eyes rested on the woman two seats ahead of me. She sat with her back to the window with a large make-up bag resting on her lap. Her extremely pale, pock-marked face reminded me of a cracked bone-china plate. Dyed, straight red hair was pulled back in a ponytail. What really caught my attention, though, was the mirror she held in her left hand.

She adroitly manipulated the mirror to help her apply her make-up. I watched as she put a foundation over her entire face using a rather large make-up sponge. Next she took out a medium-sized brush, dipped it in her container of blush, and the rich red color quickly changed her face from pale to lush.

The creak of the train car wheels and a sudden rolling movement signaled that the train was turning northwest. New rails and cars were badly needed, but money from the government never seemed to be available.

The movement didn't affect her in the least, however. Miraculously, she drew perfect black lines across her eyebrows, and applied green/gold shadow and thick black mascara. While I tumbled across the seat, this woman, as skilled as any artist, transformed small, narrow, colorless eyes into large bright beauties.

A husky booming voice coming from behind me diverted my attention: "It's your stop; wake up."

When I turned around I watched the conductor as he shook another passenger in an attempt to awaken him. The sleeper wouldn't budge, and the conductor had to leave. By the time another passenger woke up the rider, the train had hurtled on past the gentleman's stop, leaving a very distraught commuter to try to figure out how to get home.

Lucky for me, my route goes from the beginning to the end, so it would be hard for me to miss my stop. Actually, I've never been able to sleep on the train anyway, which affords me more time for people watching.

I turned my attention back to the redhead. By now she was working on her lips. Another perfect pencil line outlined her mouth, before she filled her lips in with a nice plum color. Her face was perfect—an artistic masterpiece.

The compact was put away, and she completed her outfit by unhooking her ponytail, shaking her hair out, and exchanging her flats for three-inch red heels that went very well with her short, tight black dress.

The woman who exited the train was very different than the one who had gotten on an hour earlier. I wondered who she was meeting and where she was going. It was ten o'clock Friday night, still early for the young, but not for me.

Only twenty minutes more to my trip. I leaned back and closed my eyes. Too much thinking and guessing for me in the last hour. Tomorrow was another day for people watching. As a writer I tended to spin everyone's story my way. Then again, real life stories are usually stranger than fiction, and I'll bet the drab-to-fab make-up artist has a good one.

Whether on our faces or in our minds, we all create our own art.

# Robots

Weary from a full day of shopping in downtown Chicago, I boarded my Metra train and ventured through a few cars before realizing there were no seats available without somebody already sitting next to them. So I plopped myself down next to a young blond girl. Taking off my heavy winter coat, I accidentally bumped her, knocking off her narrow, tortoise shell glasses.

"I'm sorry," I said, as I picked up the glasses and handed them to her.

She either was reluctant to make any contact or too busy texting on her cell phone to respond beyond putting the glasses back on.

The train started out, and I turned my attention to the scenery out the window. A new condo building was going up right by the station. Those strange white flowers on the pointy trees that I remembered were long gone. Replaced by cement. The expressway traffic stretched on and on. Better to be on the train. Driving in rush hour was impossible.

Large, white flakes had started to fall across the windows, making viewing difficult.

I turned to my seat companion and said, "Look out the window. It's snowing."

Annoyed, she pointed to her phone. "The meteorologists predicted snow this afternoon."

I slid down in my seat and shut up, while thinking that in my day we looked out the door or window to see what the weather was like.

After a few minutes I peered around the train car and realized I was the unusual passenger. Except for a sleeping man and one person reading a newspaper, every passenger was busy with either a computer, a cell phone, or a tablet, and most were connected to ear phones.

They were all Internet junkies. When I was working and a steady passenger on the Metra, it was very different. It used to be that the train was noisy with conversations and even card-playing. Not anymore. Lips were closed and heads were tilted down over digital devices. I bet chiropractor business had increased in the last few years. A lot of necks and shoulders probably were hurting.

No more print books were being read, there was no people watching, and no scenery-lookers or busy conversationalists were present on this train. I guess today people were afraid to engage in face-to-face dialogue.

Today the feeling is; it's safer to send a message by text or e-mail.

Strangers face-to-face are hard to un-friend, or not answer. There is always that awkward moment when one wants to end the conversation and get back to the computer without being rude. If messaging one could just say, "Gotta go."

I reached into my purse and pulled out my new mini iPad, the lighter, smaller one that was easier to carry. I might as well join the crowd. My orb, as Woody Allen would call it!

This morning I had downloaded a new book I was anxious to read.

Instead of going to the book I checked my e-mails, and people's Facebook postings first. Since I purchased this thing I found that I read less, even though I keep downloading books. It is similar to the TV remote. When in charge of it, you tend to go from station to station and never really see a full program.

"Prairie Crossing is the next stop."

The announcement caught my attention, and I thought that if the stops weren't called out most of us would ride to the end of the line before we realized we had missed ours. Actually, I had no worries. My stop was the end of the line. Then again if I fell asleep I could end up going back downtown.

I put down my iPad, sat back on the red vinyl seat, closed my eyes, and listened to the rattle of the wheels across the tracks. Suddenly the noise ceased. I opened my eyes and looked out the window. The train was stopped midway between stations.

This wasn't unusual, as Metra always managed to stop for a freight train, or some excuse, and then run a few minutes late. Initially no one paid much attention. After about fifteen minutes heads popped up in a questioning manner. One or two people actually turned to their seat-mates to see if they knew anything about the delay, since the Internet hadn't recorded anything about it yet. I once found out from social media that my train was stalled because the one ahead had hit a passenger car.

Finally, the conductor showed up and answered our queries with the patience of a man who has gone through this before.

"Sorry, but the train has a mechanical problem and everyone will be transferred to another train soon."

"When is soon?' an astute passenger asked.

"About thirty minutes," the conductor answered. Tall, thin, strong face and jaw, uniform looking as perfect now as at the beginning of the day, with the look of authority he moved on to the next car. From experience I knew we would be extremely lucky if it was only thirty minutes. Kind of like waiting in a restaurant.

Our car became alive with conversation. Heads looked up. "Did he really say thirty minutes?" "What kind of mechanical problem?"

The heat and lights in our car went off, as if we needed confirmation that the train had mechanical problems. Suddenly the snow falling outside and the fading sunlight created an ominous scene.

We got up from our seats and gathered together. We recognized our fellow passengers as beings in a common group: the stranded-on-the-train, late-for-our-appointments group.

I always carry water and cash when I venture to Chicago. Today I had the cash, but I didn't think I could buy my way off of the train. The water which was still sitting on my kitchen counter would have been nicer to have. A few cookies would also have helped since I skipped lunch today. I decided I would have to make do with my two mints; maybe they would help my dry mouth.

Speaking of buying one's way off of the train, the woman seated in front of me was calling a cab. I wasn't sure she could exit the car and walk down the tracks to a street to connect with it, but I admired her initiative. Made me wonder how we would transfer to another car. We were in a middle car Maybe there was a platform up ahead.

Problems on Metra were no surprise. Most of the trains were antiques needing so many modern things, like toilets that flush. If we were stranded too long that could be a problem. We had already been traveling over an hour.

As we waited for the new train, devices were put away and life stories were exchanged between passengers face-to-face. The car became noisy with occupants questioning and complaining to each other.

A gray-haired lady in a long black cloth coat discovered something in common with her red-headed, fur-coated seat mate.

"Did you just mention the IC on 71st street? I grew up in South Shore."

"So did I. Where did you live?"

"We lived across from O'Keefe."

"I went to school there, too. What was your maiden name?"

"Anita Levine."

"Oh my G-d, I think I used to date your brother."

I watched a salt-and-pepper-mustached man take a wrinkled photograph out of his wallet. I thought it must be a picture of his grandchildren. On closer observation I saw the picture of a brown and white sleepy eyed dog.

"Charlie is old like I am. He needs to be walked."

I handed the man my cell. "Can you call someone to help?" He shook his head in a negative gesture.

"What about my kid? He needs to be picked up at hockey practice," a younger man, sporting the Chicago Blackhawks Indian on his shirt, uttered in a worried tone while he peered out the window.

"I'm hungry," whined a cute blue-eyed four or five-year-old.

Candy, cookies, and an apple were offered to her from several generous passengers.

"What the hell happened to the lights?" a husky voice from the back of the car blurted out.

We all turned in the direction of the sound. A sleeping passenger had finally woken up.

Smiling, we realized we had been transferred from robots back to a community of human beings.

# To the South

A warm breeze scented by lilacs from the full purple bush just left of the pool deck greeted me, as I leisurely stepped out through the screen door leading from my room to the wooden deck circling above the pool. It was a perfect Southern day at the first stirrings of spring, the kind I had dreamed about through the long, cold, snow-laden Chicago winter.

The clear regal blue sky and matching pool water were enticing, but so was the white wicker couch right outside my room, and the book in my hand. I settled down, letting the warm sun caress my body, and the cold pink glass of lemonade wet my lips.

No radios blaring, no cars buzzing by, no lawn motors churning—just the melodious singing of multi-colored feathered friends hovering around the bird feeders.

I spotted the hot tub adjacent to the far end of the pool, and realized it was worth the move. I ventured down the steps towards it, climbed into the tub, and pressed the on button. The hot water bubbled and gurgled, tickling my back and feet as I sank down deep.

Upon returning to my perch on the wicker couch I found that my host had left a covered dish of Southern quiche, as well as New Orleans brioches. Too bad my husband, Sam—out on a bike trip—wasn't there to share every moment. Camellia House was a wonderful find.

We had found this charming Southern bed and breakfast by accident. A gulf cruise with our grandchildren had ended in New Orleans. They headed home, and our plans were to spend a few days in the city. Walking the streets of New Orleans was disappointing. Maybe we were just too old to enjoy the city, instead being irritated by the noise, the many odd people bumping into each other, the prostitutes, and the garbage-laden French Quarter.

We happily retired to our allegedly five-star hotel, only to discover what looked like a bed bug on the bed. Before we could determine what it was, the fire alarm went off.

We had had enough, and checked out. Sam found us a bed and breakfast in Covington, a town 25 miles to the north—a place we had planned to visit anyway because it had a famous bike path. When I travel with Sam we visit zoos, museums, dental schools (Sam's a dentist), and bike paths (he's an avid cyclist, too).

I was reluctant to go, afraid that I would miss the great New Orleans cooking I had heard so much about. But at 10 p.m. with no place to go in an overbooked city, we were lucky to find someplace close to stay.

From the moment Henry (the cabbie sent to pick us up) arrived we knew we were going back in time. Gregarious, slow talking, and eager to share charming Southern stories, he entertained us on the hour-long ride across the bridge. Then when we tried to tip him, he said, "Wait a second. I own this cab, and I'm giving you a senior discount." He reached into his pocket and gave us money back.

It turns out that Covington, Louisiana, is a charming Southern city with some of the best creole cooking in the USA. Oysters baked in a cheesy cream sauce, eggs Sardou, and crabs every way you could find them crossed our palates.

Friendly, leisurely talking folks with their Southern accents could be found everywhere. Cars stopped in the middle of the street to let us cross. All the traditions of the area were charming—long Southern porches with traditional fans, wicker rocking chairs, gorgeous pink flowers, weeping willow trees, delicious crabs and oysters, and the Camellia House—so relaxing after a busy cruise with my grandchildren.

Departure day arrived all too soon. Up early before the sun peeked over the horizon, we headed off to the airport, suitcases in hand. Once there, we learned our airplane would be delayed four hours or more, due to weather in Chicago where the winter refused to leave.

I must have a short memory, I thought. Only two weeks ago I was cursing the misery inflicted on me by the bitter cold and slippery ice-covered walks, in a city where everyone was coughing and sneezing and bundling up in sweaters and heavy coats.

Why was I so anxious to get home? I'm retired with no major commitments. The weather in southern Louisiana was fabulous, eighty degrees and sunny. The Camellia House was heavenly. I could stay here—I really could, I told myself. My palate was salivating for those tasty eggs surrounded with spinach smothered in a creamy sauce, and those wonderful crabs cooked dozens of different ways.

Home—or maybe just a lifetime of routine and commitment—was calling, and we answered. But we knew we would be back. Once you've been to Louisiana, a siren song of the South plays in your head and your soul, beckoning you until you return.

# Winter

Mother Nature's morning wake-up calls come later in the winter. Fewer vocal sounds come through the tightly sealed windows, and fewer animals are around to make them. No loud chirping or melodious mating songs are heard from the birds—just an occasional warning sound, or the honk of geese who are beginning to think Canada wasn't that bad.

Some lucky birds are vacationing in the South with some of my lucky friends. Other animals, like the skunks and chipmunks, are dug under the snow, hibernating or hiding. A faint bark from a distant dog and the persistent meow from my tabby are my wake-up calls this morning.

It takes too much effort for me to step out the door into the cold icy world. It is so much easier to hide under my warm floral comforter, but the winter blizzards and below-freezing temperatures are playing havoc with the wildlife living on the three acres outside my home. So for them, I will move from my bed.

Funny, we often care only for what we know. My first fifty years as a city girl, I never really thought about the wildlife. I took care of the pets in my world, and that was my only contact with animals.

It snowed again last night. The tree branches had only a slight reprieve before they were again covered with white. The sun is shining, making my world outside sparkle and glisten even though the thermometer still reads below zero. There are specks of red, blue, brown sitting on the branches waiting, while the bushy tailed squirrels gather any leftover seeds, and the floppy-eared bunny hides in the brush nearby.

Only to feed the animals sharing my property will I venture out in this dreadful weather. Armed with hat, heavy coat, gloves, boots, and a can full of seed, I slowly open the sliding door. A gust of cold wind makes me step back before I make it out.

The birds and squirrels have only a few moments at the feeder before a herd of deer approach. From my perch at the kitchen counter I watch the full-coated white-tailed female deer stand alert. With ears high and bright black eyes, they scan the area for danger as their young busily devour the seeds.

When the deer leave, the birds return. The fluttering of wings from the trees to the bird feeders has an order similar to the line at the deli counter. The mating sky-dances and territorial fighting are months away.

I am secure in my winter solitude, especially this year. Though I am given to complaints, I realize I am blessed with retirement and can stay home, and watch the winter world that features my little friends continue on from my window.

# Without a Phone!

I walked out of the house without my mobile phone. I didn't even have an iPad on me. It is 2015 and I walked out without my cell, and I never discovered it missing until I was at least 15 minutes down the road. Had I been closer to home I would have turned my car around and retrieved it.

Once I discovered the phone was missing, I panicked. I wasn't just traveling to the nearest grocery story. I was planning to spend hours out, going at least 40 miles to meet a friend for lunch. I felt completely disconnected from the world.

The first thing I did was to stop at a gas station. God forbid my car would run out of gas while I was traveling without my cell. The thought of being stranded somewhere without communication was too much to bear.

I went into the ladies room and emptied my purse to make sure the phone wasn't hiding somewhere in it. No luck. It was nowhere in the purse, or in my pockets.

When I came out of the rest room I scanned the station for a public phone. Of course there was none. Nobody uses a public phone—nor does anyone have a landline in their home anymore.

I found myself driving more cautiously than before. God forbid I would have a car accident without my phone. Then I realized if I continued to drive at this slow pace I would be late for lunch, and without a cell phone I couldn't call my friend, so I speeded up. Thank God I knew how to navigate to my destination. My car wasn't equipped with a GPS.

I thought about my husband. He was out on a bicycle ride. If he needed me there was no way he could find me. Then again I was too far away to help him anyway.

Then I realized ADT Security couldn't contact me in case my house was burglarized, or burned down. Did I leave the dryer on, or the toaster plugged into the outlet?

Maybe I was traveling this far for nothing. My friend could be trying to call or message me to cancel the date. What other emails or messages was I missing? How frustrating to be in the dark.

Oh, how could I be so careless? It must be my age, or my hormones. I've never done this before. I once left my wallet home, but then I had my phone to call my husband and he brought it to me.

My heart was racing as I tightly gripped the steering wheel. I should have gone back and just been late. Now I will have to drive home in the dark without the mobile. The weather station even predicted rain. I will just have to shorten our lunch date.

Finally I pulled into the shopping center. I let out a sigh of relief when my car was parked. I made sure my auto was locked, and I scanned the parking lot for stranger danger. I use to carry a whistle and a flashlight, but there was no need for those things now that I have the new digital devices—except for today when my digital devices are at home.

When I entered the restaurant, I ran up to my friend and blurted out, "I'm a wreck. I drove here without my cell phone. I left it home."

She smiled at me. "No big deal. You made it through your first 60 years without a mobile phone. You can make it through a day."

I was relieved by her calm logical advice—that is until she answered her ringing cell.

Every once in a while we get tested by life, but that doesn't mean we should expect our friends to take the test with us.

# Senior Moments

# A Letter to my Parents from a Woman Approaching Seventy

I understand now.

I understand now: Why you wanted to tell me stories about your youth and my ancestors. I only wish I had listened and asked you more questions.

I understand now: Why you repeated the same stories over and over. My friends hold up their fingers to let me know how many times I've told them the same story. Sometimes they run out of fingers.

I understand now: Why you said, "Don't try to take my car away. I only drive on roads I know." My own eyes and reflexes have slowed down, but I have no problem driving on the roads that *I* know.

I understand now: Why you read the obituaries in the newspaper, and took a comforting breath when you found no one you knew.

I understand now: Why you kept so much stuff. You should see my garage and basement today.

I understand now: Why when you went out with friends the two men sat in the front seat and the two women sat in the back.

I understand now: Why you talked so much about your aches and pains, and how much your medicine cost.

I understand now: Why your hands trembled, and you dropped things. My friends now call me "Shaky."

I understand now: Why you talked about people and places that haven't existed for years. Singers like Al Jolson; places like Fidelman's in South Haven, Michigan; or restaurants like Ashkenaz. I reminisce about Elvis Presley, the Nippersink resort, and the Rascal House deli.

I understand now: Why you refused to learn how to use the VCR. You wouldn't believe the electronics I have to try to work today.

I understand now: Why you hated to go out in the ice and snow. Broken toes and broken ribs heal much more slowly when you are older.

I understand now: Why you forgot names, and mixed up places.

I understand now: Why you almost burned down the house while cooking. I just don't bother cooking any longer.

I understand now: Why you napped.

I understand now: Why, though you dressed with care, by the end of the day your clothes had a few food stains.

I understand now: Why you couldn't keep up with my pace when we walked.

I understand now: Why you tired so after playing with your grandchildren, even though you loved being with them.

I understand now: Why you sometimes forgot why you went into a room.

I understand now: Why you had so much time, after spending a lifetime of being busy and always in a hurry.

I understand now: Why you no longer criticized me when I made a mistake.

I understand now: Why you constantly told me that you loved me.

I understand now: Why you let me win at Kalookie.

I understand now: Why you said, "Don't buy me gifts—just be sure to remember me with a call, a card, and a hug."

I understand now: Why you just smiled when I disregarded experience and acted like I knew better than you did.

I understand now: Why you said, "Keep things in perspective. Know the difference between a slight problem and real trouble."

I understand now: Why you believed that the important things in life are love, health, friendship, and respect—not money and power.

I understand now: Why you quoted the old Jewish saying: "Man plans, and God laughs!"

# Cricket?

Were you ever annoyed by the sound a cricket makes? It is a loud, annoying chirp.

My sister and I shared a bedroom when we were young. I was a pretty sound sleeper until she made me aware of the crickets outside our window. Sixty years later those darn crickets can still make me crazy, so you should understand my horror when I approached my kitchen sink and a large chirping sound emitted from it.

Knocking on the sink made the noise louder. When I looked down the drain with a flashlight, I thought I saw something moving. I was sure it was a cricket. I put a string down the sink thinking maybe the bug would climb up. The noise continued, but nothing climbed out of the sink.

My whole day was ruined. How could I cook for Mother's Day when an annoying cricket was stuck in the sink? I didn't know what to do. Then my sister called, and my dilemma became disastrous.

I put the phone near the drain for her to listen to the sound. "That is not a cricket," she declared. "It must be a small animal caught in the pipe. Be careful."

This came from the sister who knew the sound of crickets since she was a little girl. I panicked. I better try to drown it, I thought. I ran hot water down the drain. The chirping sound only increased. Now I was feeling guilty. Some poor living thing was in distress and I was only making its pain worse. I turned the water off.

A friend called. I let her listen to the sound. She suggested I call a plumber. Another friend thought someone from wildlife control would be a better idea.

The annoying chirping continued. It was Sunday. I may have trouble getting someone out, I thought, as I checked the Internet.

My husband came home just as I was dialing an emergency twenty-four hour plumber.

"Sam, help!" I said. "There is a cricket or some animal stuck in the drain. Listen to the chirping."

He followed the sound to the sink.

"It does sound like a cricket, but I really think it's the bird," he said.

"What bird?" I asked.

"The one sitting on the ledge above the drain," Sam said, matter-of-factly. "I bought it at the dollar store yesterday."

I think I was set up. Sam says no. I couldn't be that dumb, could I?

# Help

"Help, I've fallen and I can't get up," I yelled. *Oh My God I sound like that silly commercial,* I thought.

I took a deep breath, leaned my right hand on the pink tile floor of the bathroom, and tried to pick myself up. An excruciating pain radiated down my hip and through my leg, making it impossible for me to move. Hot, wet tears flowed down my face. I wiped my eyes with my left hand. The slightest movement felt like someone was sticking big, sharp, serrated knives into me.

Okay, time to assess my situation. I had taken a bath in my enormous beautiful pink tub with the Jacuzzi, and had slipped on the floor on the way out. It was a stupid of me to take that bath before leaving for the airport. It was the thought of spending a week in hotel showers—and I had to change my clothes anyway, right?—that lured me into the tub.

That darn hand shaking gets me in trouble all the time. Earlier, I went and spilled spaghetti sauce on my blouse. I should have thrown out the leftovers. My mother had done a number on me decades ago. Starving children syndrome.

Damn, it hurts to even move my head. My whole right side is in bad shape. Too bad I don't have that thing around my neck from the commercial. I wonder if it really works?

"Ring!" went my cell phone—a nice, loud siren coming from the adjoining bedroom. Can't miss it. I heard my friend Sally's rasping voice, which was getting harder and harder to understand. I must make her go to the doctor and get it checked. She always used to have a soft, gentle sound.

"Annie, have a great time at the conference," I heard her say.

"Help, help!" I screamed. The phone went dead. Why hadn't I taken the cell or landline phone into the bathroom with me? Oh, what's the difference—with my luck I would have dropped it in the water and gotten electrocuted.

I really miss Jack. If he hadn't died I wouldn't be alone in this house. Now, I can scream all day and no one will hear me. If a tree falls in the forest and no one is there, does it make a noise? It sure does. The closest neighbor is two acres away and all my friends think I'm on my way to a writing conference in California. Not like the old days when we lived in apartments on top of each other and everybody knew when you took a pee.

My only hope is a burglar, though he would probably steal the necklace off of me, plus everything else in the house and leave me sitting here to die.

Even the cat went and died on me. What good would the cat be anyway? He would just run away and hide. Cats are smart. They take care of themselves first. Now if I had a dog he would stay and go down with the ship with me. Stupid dogs. Too loyal.

Speaking of going down with the ship, I never turned the tub faucet off, and that water is getting high. Jack, my husband—may he rest in peace—always told me if I didn't learn to swim I'd drown in the pool. I'll show him; I'll drown in the bathroom instead.

I can see the headlines: "Crazy old lady leaves the tub water flowing and drowns." I remember when my grandmother forgot to turn the tub water off, and the bathroom flooded. The neighbor downstairs came upstairs screaming about the water coming through her ceiling. She and my dad yelled at each other for at least 20 minutes, which wasn't unusual since my dad and the neighbor were brother and sister. It was the family building. Now, everyone lives in a different state. But they have Facebook to connect them, which certainly doesn't help when the tub is overflowing.

Nobody will notice me gone. A few birds might be upset; no food in the feeders. My daughter will keep saying, "I told her to sell the house and go into a retirement place, where someone would check on her all the time." Moving hadn't helped my mother-in-law. She died sometime during the night. They found her sitting upright with the television on and the remote in her hand. I still wonder what television program gave her that heart attack. But they found her relatively quickly. I could be lying here dead for a week. Dead is dead!

I really miss Jack. Though once the grief receded, I must admit it hasn't been that bad being mistress of my own life—getting up and going to bed at my leisure, eating whatever pleases me, spending money without scrutiny.

The water is slipping over the tub. It is cold, too. Yes, I could die. I started to laugh. My mother always told me to wear clean underwear in case I was in an accident. When they rescue me they will find a naked, wrinkled, flabby old lady without clean underwear, and my mother will be mortified, even in the afterlife. Maybe I could reach the soft blue towel to cover me.

Ah, oh, my God, I can't move. The pain is bad. Maybe I broke something. I reach out and touch the soaked towel. I try, but I can't move it closer. With all that water, it weighs a ton.

If I knew I was going to die tonight, what would I have done differently— call my family and friends and tell them how much I loved them? Actually, I probably would have cleaned up the house so they wouldn't say "look at this mess," and then I would eat all the chocolate I could find. A nice cup of coffee or hot chocolate would be wonderful now. If I made it to the writing conference I could just call room service. Too bad.

Who knows what I would have done? One never believes something tragic will happen to them. That is why we slow down for traffic at an accident, or listen intently to the news. "Look what happened to them; thank God it wasn't me!" We can think that, but we don't ever say it to anybody.

Nobody is going to rescue me. Most of my friends are dead, and the living ones can't drive at night. There have been too many funerals when you make it to your eighties. It is up to me to move towards the door and rescue myself.

Again the phone rang. I swallowed hard as I listened to the message from my neighbor, "Oh, Anna, I forgot you were going to a conference."

I screamed," No, no, I need help. Please come over." The phone went dead. Why was I screaming? If Mildred were sitting next to me she couldn't hear anyway. The woman never wore her hearing aid. The one she told everyone cost her son a fortune.

I shivered as I watched the round bar of white soap slip over the tub with the cascading water, like a boat going over a waterfall. Kind of neat looking, actually.

Okay, focus on your situation, I tell myself. The question is, will I drown, or just die of pain, or starvation? My mother always said, "If there is a will, there is a way." She also said, "Man plans, and God laughs."

I looked up through the window and asked, "So God, are you laughing?" An enormous boom answered my question. Maybe it was my plane flying by. A flash of lightning confirmed it was thunder. A second rumble made the curtains in the window flutter from the vibration. At least I won't have to water the lawn, I thought. If this storm keeps up, though, the lights will probably go out. I'd better make my move.

Sharp shards of pain flooded my body as I slowly inched towards the door. I reached my trembling hand up to open the gold, round handle and stopped. If I opened the door the water would flow into my bedroom and ruin my carpet.

*Crazy old lady*, I said to myself. Die or ruin the carpet? It is an interesting question. I've had a pretty good 82 years, and the carpet was relatively new. Got that new blue carpet when Jack died. He wouldn't get it. Always said nobody will buy a house with blue carpet.

Then I thought of my grandchildren, and with all my energy I turned the knob and pushed open the door. Just a little slide more would put me in reach of my cell phone. 911 here I come!

Wet carpet or no, I decided to live. After all, what a great story this would make at the *next* writing conference!

# I Need A Book (I Really Do)

I need a book; I really do.

I need a book; I really do: I want to hold and cuddle those paper pages anew. I want to flip through from page one to page 902.

I need a book; I really do: I want to be able to quickly check information. The thought of no book is giving me vexation.

I need a book; I really do: I don't care if the print is small, too. I'll adjust; I always do.

I need a book; I really do: So the pages are yellow and brittle to the touch. The pages number 102, and I've re-read them almost as much.

I need a book; I really do: So it weighs much more than digital devices; what a sin. But it is always there and never needs to be plugged in.

I need a book; I really do: Books get lost, you say. But tell me, has anyone really retrieved lost text from the cloud, anyway?

I need a book; I really do: With pencil in hand I scribble notes all over the pages. Yes, I must admit I sometimes deface a favorite book with both admiration and rages.

I need a book; I really do: One I can share with my grandchild. Just try telling an Internet bed-time story without getting riled.

I need a book; I really do: They make a great booster seat. And under a projector, they are neat.

I need a book; I really do: My bookshelves are empty, gathering dust. Who will say, with so many books, be an intellectual she must?

I need a book; I really do: When the electricity is out, worthless are my Kindle, iPad, and Nook. Just give me a candle and a book.

I need a book; I really do: As a famous writer (ha-ha) my books will still be around for many views. Long after today's digital devices go the way of yesterday's news.

I need a book; I really do: One or two, that I can pass on to you!

# If You Wake Up Tomorrow and I Am Gone

If you wake up tomorrow and I am gone
Cry a little but not too much, because life only allows each of us so many
steps before the fall.

If you wake up tomorrow and I am gone
Shed tears of grief and tears of laughter when you think of me.

If you wake up tomorrow and I am gone
Remember me young, thin, and free.
Remember me old, fat, and gray.
Just remember me.

If you wake up tomorrow and I am gone
There will be many things we didn't say, but understand not everything
needed to be spoken.

If you wake up tomorrow and I am gone
Keep me in your heart, but carry on, for you surely know how precious and
how short life can be.

If you wake up tomorrow and I am gone
Don't make me a saint just because I'm no more. We all have our flaws.
They are the special things that make us human.

If you wake up tomorrow and I am gone
Please keep the tales going that bring a tear to your eye, and the ones that
bring a sly grin to your lips. I want my grandkids to know all sides of
me.

If you wake up tomorrow and I am gone
Please keep the stories I have written, and the pictures I've saved.
Keep the memories of who I was, and the ones that define who you are in the
scheme of the family tree.

If you wake up tomorrow and I am gone
Each of you will remember me in a different way, because you have loved me
or not loved me, and I have touched your soul or not.

If you wake up tomorrow and I am gone
Remember I have loved you in my way.

# Senior Shopping

My husband, Sam, and I left the van, and walked together into the Walgreens drugstore. Then we separated, Sam taking his cart, and me taking mine.

Since we retired, shopping has become a battlefield between us. Sam buys anything on sale whether we need it or not, and I only buy what I want. If it is on sale that is a bonus, but I really don't care.

After numerous battles we've devised a plan. We become strangers in the store, only to meet back at the van, hiding our purchases from each other until we arrive home.

Usually I'm back at the van way before he is, but on this day I lingered in the card section. When I made it to the register I was the only one in line. A friendly young girl was ringing up my purchases. I was facing her when a man behind me started to load the counter with his abundant merchandise. When the clerk told me my account had a ten dollar credit, without missing a beat or turning around I pointed behind me and said, "Give it to him."

The clerk's mouth fell open. "What did you say, you want to give $10 to a stranger? Give it to me then!"

I started to laugh, as I said. "He's my husband. We have to shop separately."

She raised her eyebrows in a curious gesture, and said, "Whatever you say."

I'm not sure she really believed me as I exited without him, but had she looked out the window, she'd have seen me giving Sam a peck on the cheek. Maybe she thought I'd come up with a clever new way to pick up guys!

# Senior Travel

As I assessed my fellow cruise travelers, I realized we were between the ages of 60 and 80. Most of us were retired professionals, businesspeople, or prominent leaders in our professions, who were having a hard time relinquishing our positions to younger people. This made for lively conversations.

We are seasoned travelers who have been on many different trips.

We have the money and the time to travel, but we sleep on the bus, and can hardly see, hear, or walk on the tours. There are more canes, walkers, and wheelchairs than I've seen on other trips. We are troupers who tread carefully, as many of us already have gone the route of replacement hips and knees.

We really come alive during meals. We eat heartily while comparing the quality of the food against that of other ships. We love to reminisce with our contemporaries about how it used to be. We have all the new cell phones, iPads, and other digital devices; we carry them along, but we still prefer books, newspapers, radios, televisions, and the opinions of each other.

As passengers we come from all over the world. Most of us are Americans, but there are a lot of Britons and we have a good time mis-speaking the same language to each other. We laugh a lot while sipping wine.

We dress nicely, but conservatively, paying more attention to comforts:

extra sweaters for the chill in the air, umbrellas just in case, shoes that are good for walking. We carry shopping bags, but buy little as our homes are already stacked with tons of things our children don't want. Although, if we are taken to a shop with goodies for our grandchildren, we come alive.

We take a million pictures that we will never identify once we arrive home. It really won't matter, because in the long run we or our children will end up deleting them from our cameras or computers.

We are trying to see the world before we leave it, now that we can enjoy it at a slower pace, and access what we see with the knowledge of experience and history.

Before we ourselves become history.

# When I'm Gone

I've often wondered why the leaves on the trees are at their prettiest right before they fall off and die. The explosion of burnt red next to a brilliant yellow- and green-dressed tree is spectacular. When the green blood of life fades and the leaves wither through their last days, the world recognizes them. Pictures are taken, stories are written, and passersby walk with their eyes toward the sky, admiring the colorful scene.

Not so with us humans. When the young die they are still beautiful and so honored, but not us old souls. Our beauty is long gone; we have lingered too long, and are usually tossed to the wind.

With this in mind, I've decided to plan my own funeral. You see, I've passed into my seventies, and so many of my closest friends and favorite family members have died before me. I've been to enough funerals to know what I like—and what I don't.

I realize it is very important to have the best picture available put into the obituaries. It doesn't matter if I am 102; the picture must present me as a beauty queen. After spending weeks going through pictures, I've picked out one of me feeding my dog an ice-cream cone. The dog is adorable, and at age two, with curly black hair, I was also kind of cute.

I've picked out my casket. It is blue, blue, blue, my favorite color. Dress me in one of my size 8 St. John's, no matter if I weigh 202. And don't forget the sweater. I'm always cold. Oh yes, pink lipstick even if my face is ashen white.

Today everyone must have a platform, and their say-so. Well, I really hate to listen to five to ten friends or new acquaintances get up and praise a bastard to all heaven. So when it is your turn to talk about me, let it out. If you hate me, don't praise me. Tell the world all the terrible things I did, back when. Just don't you dare tell me when I'm still here. Keep pretending I'm great!

None of that crazy seven-day Shiva, with the mirrors covered, and the house as quiet as a mouse. Have a party. Have a catered party, with a band. Serve salmon, beef, rolls, cheese, kugels, chopped liver, cookies, and all kinds of cake. Have the band play Johnny Mathis, Elvis Presley, and a cha cha for my husband, Sam.

Have a scavenger hunt. Try to find where I've hidden all the jewels. Go through my pockets and you will find enough money to pay for the funeral, because there won't be much left in my estate, as I've spent it all on frivolous material things and luxury vacations.

I'm still working on putting something interesting on my tombstone. Maybe my granddaughter can write a special poem.

Bury me next to my son. He's been waiting for me.

Remember, we've all been sentenced to death for a crime we haven't committed, so keep in mind that you will join me soon

So don't rush. Enjoy every minute you are alive!

# About the Author

Charlene Wexler is a graduate of the University of Illinois. She has worked as a teacher and dental office bookkeeper and as "a wife, mom, and grandmother," she said. In recent years, Wexler's lifelong passion for writing has led her to create numerous essays as well as fiction.

She is the author of the books *Lori, Murder Across the Ocean, Murder on Skid Row, Milk and Oranges,* and *Elephants In The Room.*

Her work has appeared in several publications, including *North Shore Magazine;* the University of Illinois at Chicago College of Dentistry's *Vision* magazine; *Alpha Omegan* magazine; the book and CD *Famous Poets of the Heartland: A Treasury of Beloved Family Poems,* Talent, OR: Famous Poets Press, 2014; and the *Gazette* newspaper of Chicago.

She also has had essays and fiction published on the websites AuthorsDen.com, The Best Short Stories, Booksie.com, Classic Short Stories, Cat Stories, Cats and Dogs at Play, End Your Sleep Deprivation.com, Funny Cat Stories, Funny Cats Playing, Funny Passport Stories, How Old is Grandma?, Laughter Is My Medicine, Make-Up Mouse, Moral Short Stories-Ethical Tales, One Bright Star.org, Scribd.com, Short Stories for Women, Short-Stories.net, True Cat Stories, Way Cool Dogs.com, and the Write City Magazine.

Poetry of Wexler's appears on Poetry.com.

Wexler's first novel, *Murder on Skid Row,* was published in 2010. It is the story of a double-murder on Chicago's Skid Row in the 1960s. *Murder on Skid Row* won an international Apex Award of Excellence from Communications Concepts, a writing think tank outside Washington, DC.

Published as an e-book on Smashwords and as a print edition by Central Park Communications in 2012, *Milk and Oranges,* is a collection of her short fiction and essays examining life, love, and the tragedy and comedy of the human condition. Whether she is tackling fiction or essays, Wexler writes from the heart. With a keen eye for detail and a way of looking at the world a bit sideways, Wexler's writings in *Milk and Oranges* entertain while they make you think.

*Milk and Oranges* received a Bronze Award in the Women's Issues category of the eLit Book Awards competition sponsored by the publishing services firm Jenkins Group Inc. of Traverse City, MI, and a rare international Grand Award in the Apex Awards competition by Communications Concepts in 2012.

In 2014, Charlene published two novels as e-books on Smashwords and Amazon Kindle: *Lori,* a family saga spanning several decades, and *Murder Across the Ocean,* a murder mystery set in England. *Murder Across the Ocean* also is available from Amazon as a paperback.

Her short story *Abracadabra Magic* received a "Very Highly Commended" rating in the AuthorsDen.com Tom Howard Prose Contest, 2009.

Wexler is active with the Alpha Omega Dental Fraternity, the Authors Marketing Group, the Chicago Writers Association, Children's Memorial Hospital philanthropy, the Geneva Lake Museum, Literary Fiction Writers, the Love is Murder Conference, Lungevity (an organization that fights lung cancer), the McHenry Bicycle Club, the Museum of Science and Industry, the Mystery Writers of America, the National Council of Jewish Women, the Richmond IL Book Club, Sisters in Crime, the Jewish United Fund, and the University of Illinois Alumni Association.

She is on Facebook and Twitter.

"I have always used writing as therapy," Wexler said. "Now I have the time and opportunity to pursue it as a career."

Her advice for other aspiring writers—even grandmothers like herself—is to "follow your dream. You can do it, and it's never too late."

# Connect with Charlene Wexler

Facebook: facebook.com/Charlene.wexler
LinkedIn: https://www.linkedin.com/in/charlene-wexler-0ba88b30
Twitter: twitter.com/search?q=Charlene+Wexler
Website: charlenewexler.com

# Books by Charlene Wexler

*Elephants In The Room*
*Lori*
*Milk and Oranges*
*Murder Across the Ocean*
*Murder on Skid Row*

# Permissions

"A Day in the Life of a Chicago Teenager, 1959" and "Autograph Book" reprinted courtesy of the website Booksie.com.

"A Letter to my Parents" reprinted courtesy of *The Write City.*

"A Night in an Inner City Hospital" reprinted courtesy of Short-Story.net.

"Apple Strudel" reprinted courtesy of the website How Old is Grandma? http://www.guy-sports.com/months/jokes_grandma.htm.

"Battleground: Leftovers" and "Lights, Camera, Catharsis" reprinted courtesy of the website Short Stories for Women, http://www.guy-sports.com/humor/stories/short_stories_women.htm.

"Cat-ching On" reprinted courtesy of the website Cats and Dogs at Play, http://www.guy-sports.com/humor/videos/cats_dogs.htm.

"Charlie, Our Therapist" reprinted courtesy of the website Way Cool Dogs.com, http://www.waycooldogs.com/charlie-the-therapist/.

"Help" reprinted courtesy of the website Moral Short Stories-Ethical Tales, http://www.guy-sports.com/humor/stories/moral_short_stories.htm#Help_By_Charlene_Wexler.

"Hilltop Winter" reprinted courtesy of the website The Best Short Stories, http://www.guy-sports.com/humor/stories/best_short_stories.htm.

# Photo Credits

Cover: Cartoon by Chuck Senties.

*Coming of Age*
A Day in the Life of a Chicago Teenager, 1959: Wikimedia Commons Public Domain.
It was the 'Fifties: Charlene Wexler collection.
Second Date: Chance Agrella, photo courtesy of and copyright Free Range Stock, www.freerangestock.com.
Taking Nothing for Granted: Charlene Wexler collection.

*Family and Friends*
A Night in an Inner City Hospital: Mark Wanger, Freeimages.com.
Apple Strudel: Che, Wikimedia Commons Public Domain.
Aunt Millie: Charlene Wexler collection.
The Autograph Book: Charlene Wexler collection.
Elephants In The Room: Chuck Senties.
The Gates Are About to Close: Chance Agrella, photo courtesy of and copyright Free Range Stock, www.freerangestock.com.
The Hoarder Gene: Charlene Wexler collection.
Loss and Grief: Yanir, photo courtesy of and copyright Free Range Stock, www.freerangestock.com.
No More Free Pie: Eric Yuen, photo courtesy of and copyright Free Range Stock, www.freerangestock.com.
Spiritual Connection? Nikolya Magukiov, Freeimages.com.
The Temperature Games: ClipArtHut.com.
The Treasure: Charlene Wexler collection.

*Animal Magnetism*

Charlie, Our Therapist: Charlene Wexler collection.

Into the Woods: Charlene Wexler collection.

Ode to Tyrone: Charlene Wexler collection.

Tyrone is No More: Charlene Wexler collection.

There Is a Frog in my Pool: Charlene Wexler collection.

Feeding a Stray Kitten that I Really Don't Need: Charlene Wexler collection.

*The Passing Parade*

The Congress to Make Humans: Blue Sky, Freeimages.com.

Hilltop Winter: Photo courtesy of and copyright Free Range Stock, www.freerangestock.com.

The Metra Train: Charlene Wexler collection.

To the South: Charlene Wexler collection.

Winter: Charlene Wexler collection.

Without a Phone! Jack Moreh, photo courtesy of and copyright Free Range Stock, www.freerangestock.com.

*Senior Moments*

A Letter to my Parents from a Woman Approaching Seventy: Marcel Hol, Freeimages.com.

Cricket? Jared Davidson, photo courtesy of and copyright Free Range Stock, www.freerangestock.com.

I Need A Book: Amanda Mills, www.public-domain-image.com

If You Wake Up Tomorrow and I Am Gone: Lauren Lank, Freeimages.com.

Senior Shopping: www.public-domain-image.com.

Senior Travel: Andre Seitz, Freeimages.com.

When I'm Gone: www.public-domain-image.com.